THREE

THREE

noelle mack

KENSINGTON PUBLISHING CORP.
http://www.kensingtonbooks.com

APHRODISIA books are published by

Kensington Publishing Corp.
850 Third Avenue
New York, NY 10022

All Kensington Titles, Imprints, and Distributed Lines are available at special quantity discounts for bulk purchases for sales promotions, premiums, fund-raising, educational or institutional use.

Special book excerpts or customized printings can also be created to fit specific needs. For details, write or phone the office of the Kensington special sales manager: Kensington Publishing Corp., 850 Third Avenue, New York, NY 10022, attn: Special Sales Department, Phone: 1-800-221-2647.

ISBN 0-7582-1389-1

First Kensington Trade Paperback Printing: January 2006

10 9 8 7 6 5 4 3 2 1

Printed in the United States of America

For JWR, with pleasure . . .

1

Black velvet suited her, Fiona thought, looking in the mirror with the faintest of smiles. And the lustrous triple strand of pearls around her throat provided a demure touch of white. She touched them with a fingertip, then pulled her rumpled gown back down over her bare thighs and legs as her naked and muscular companion bent down to kiss the nape of her neck. She laughed and tipped her head to one side, allowing him, inviting him, to dally with her once more.

He slid his hands inside the front of her gown and over her breasts, tugging gently at her nipples as he whispered into her ear. "My dear lady, I am sorry to leave you. But I must."

"Then do not delay," Fiona said calmly. "And give your wayward wife my fondest regards." She removed his hands and sat upon the small armchair placed before the mirror, taking down her honey-colored hair pin by pin, in no great hurry. It tumbled free over her shoulders.

"I shall," Thomas sighed, standing in back of her and running his fingers through the glossy locks. "If I can persuade her to leave her lover's arms long enough to come downstairs."

"Do you permit her to entertain the fellow in your house?"

"It is her house," he pointed out. "And she does whatever she wants. I don't care. I have all the freedom a man could wish for. She has never asked where I was going or when I might return."

Fiona nodded. "Then you are fortunate." She rose from her dressing table, unclasping the pearls and coiling them in a tortoiseshell box with an open lid. Dear Thomas. He did not have to know that she had several necklaces very like this one, hidden in other elegant boxes and silk bags.

He frowned. "Must you take them off? I rather fancied the idea of you wearing nothing but the gems of the ocean, like Aphrodite, rolling about in the billows—or should I say pillows? It is nearly midnight, you know. Sleep with the pearls on."

"Since you will not be here to see how I look, what does it matter?"

He clasped her around the waist and kissed her on the cheek. "The moon will see you. And I will see the moon on my way home and it will tell me how beautiful you are."

"You are being ridiculously romantic."

"Not at all." He kissed her again, long and tenderly, capturing her mouth with his, and not stopping for at least a minute.

She broke away at last. "Ah. How you can kiss, Thomas."

"I have had some talented teachers. Including you, Fiona." He kissed her again and looked down at his stiffening cock. "We might have another go. Would you like to?"

"Of course," she lied. "But I was going to bathe before bed. The maid will be bringing up the hot water soon."

Thomas laughed. "Wonderful! I can imagine you wet and naked!" He put his hand between her legs and gave a rude squeeze. "And ready for . . . soft lips upon lips that are softer still. I know how much you like to have your cunny licked, my sweet."

"Mmm."

"Is that all you have to say? Merely mmm? Then I shan't let you come right away. Imagine my tongue sliding deeply into you, Fiona. In and out. In and out. Like a cock. One that cannot come and only wants to delight you."

"Mmm," she said again with considerably more enthusiasm. She could almost be tempted, especially by that scenario.

Thomas clasped her again beneath the velvet. "You could close your eyes and imagine that the infamous Lady Raynald has her head between your legs. I understand that she is considered an expert in Sapphic skills."

"I have heard that she is an expert horsewoman as well," Fiona said, "and rich enough to indulge her unusual tastes."

"And what are those?"

"She likes brothel girls of twenty or so. By that age many are weary of men and quite prefer their own sex. She pays for two at a time and they undress . . . and kiss . . . and embrace . . . while she fondles and teases their plump cunnies." Fiona ran a brush through her hair, humming idly. "She prefers them to be shaved there."

"Pretty peaches, dripping juice . . . what else?"

Fiona twisted her hair around one hand and studied herself in the mirror, amused by his impatience. The best way to tell such a story was slow-w-w-ly.

"Fiona, you are a dreadful tease!"

She touched his bare buttocks affectionately with the bristly part of the brush. "One naked girl straddles the other, gripping tightly with her thighs, and . . ."

Thomas put his hands on his narrow hips and tried to glare the rest out of her. "And what?"

"Lady Raynald gives them riding lessons. With a crop. Then they service her as she desires. They kneel in turn to lick her pussy, after begging their stern mistress for the privilege."

"How delightfully perverse."

Fiona waved a hand airily. "And then, of course, she straps on a large dildo for their pleasure."

"How ingenious," Thomas said. "But I should like to see the horseplay most of all. Do the girls neigh?" He smirked, obviously in need of a smack, which Fiona supplied, with the smooth side of the brush. "Ow!"

"You deserved it."

"I did not. I was merely expressing a healthy curiosity."

"Then inquire at Mrs. Quaintree's establishment. They offer bareback riding as a specialty. I believe it is near Covent Garden—you could ask a friend."

"Never. You are all that I desire. Now, what was I saying?"

"You were telling me how you would go about licking me," she said patiently.

"Ah, yes. I want to see you open your legs all the way so that I can see inside the juicy folds. You may touch yourself with a finger for a little while but not for long."

"Then what?"

"I haven't decided. Perhaps I shall spread those beautiful legs of yours myself and tie those pretty ankles far apart so my tongue can go far up inside you."

"Indeed." She smiled demurely. "But not now."

"Ah, well."

Her indifference seemed to wilt him—or perhaps it was the sudden chiming of the clock, reminding him of his duty to his bitch of a wife, Fiona thought.

"Next time, then, my dear lady. I look forward to it." He almost bowed, then remembered that he was naked and gave her a rueful grin.

"As do I."

"Then promise me, Fiona," he began, slipping first one leg and then the other into the breeches he picked up from the floor.

"You know that I do not make promises."

"I was only going to ask that you wear my gift a little longer. Those damned pearls cost me a small fortune."

"Well," she said lightly, "if it means that much to you, then I will wear them in my bath. And to bed. And to breakfast. And all through the day until I see you again."

"Thank you." He took the pearls from the box and clasped them once more about her throat, fumbling a little. "Then I know you will be thinking of me."

Fiona raised an elegant eyebrow. "Of course."

"Is that so much to ask? I love you."

She shook her head. "You shouldn't. I am a thoroughly wicked woman, according to your dear mama, the countess. She said as much to me at Almack's when she thought no one was listening."

"Oh, dear," Thomas said. "I expect she thinks I ought to spend more time at home and sire a few grandchildren. But my wife is not likely to produce any that look like me."

Fiona stroked his hair. "Why did you marry Anne? She is far from beautiful and never faithful."

Thomas shrugged. "Her dowry. Her parents let it be known that a considerable sum would be awarded to the suitablest gentleman of pure pedigree, as they put it, so that their darling daughter could marry up. They hoped to rub elbows with the gentry themselves."

"How romantic," Fiona said dryly.

"Isn't it?" He took her by the waist and twirled her around. "I much prefer your company, my naughty angel."

"Did you ever love her?"

"Certainly not. And as far as the marriage, I had very little choice in the matter. My forebears had a bad habit of burning through money. Gambling, extravagant living, mistresses—" he chucked Fiona under the chin—"that sort of thing."

"I see," she said. "Then you ought not to give me trinkets, Thomas."

"Pshaw. You deserve those pearls. As I was saying, I married Anne because my family's London house costs the deuce to keep up and Mama has two in the country to maintain as well. In fact, the roof at Castleward has sprung a number of leaks this very spring and I must—"

She shot him an impatient look. "You must place pots and pans in strategic places upon the floor, Thomas. Return home, my lord. You have done what you came to do, and I pronounce myself well satisfied."

Her lover grinned and fastened his breeches, looking about for his boots.

"Over there." Fiona pointed. The boots had been hastily pulled off and flung into a corner. He could have done the honors with them on and his breeches partway down, like any other man, she supposed. But Thomas preferred to be quite naked, though he usually insisted that she keep on some of her clothes.

Tonight he had lifted her black velvet gown up to her waist and yanked down her lace-trimmed drawers a second later, revealing her bottom, which he had stroked tenderly—at first. He'd kneeled to kiss both soft cheeks all over, spreading them so he could see everything, then stood up to administer tingling slaps from his strong hands, keeping her bent over the bed, quite unable to do anything but enjoy herself until he thrust deeply inside her.

She was positively glowing from his attentions to that part of her body. And her nipples were still tight and hard. Once he had turned her round and got rid of her drawers, he had freed her breasts from her lowcut gown and let them bounce in his hands while he rammed his thick cock, well roped with veins and slick, into her again and again. He had tugged on her erect nipples for good measure, in an irregular rhythm that excited her into a second climax soon after her first.

Still, the gown had ripped under the sleeve. Thomas was

nothing if not virile, but his preferred mode of lovemaking was hell on clothes.

He set about retrieving the rest of his own attire rather quickly, as married men were wont to do, Fiona thought to herself. But he dressed carelessly, having no need to put on a show of propriety for his straying wife. He left his shirt untucked and went to the window to look out—a precaution, Fiona supposed, to avoid an angry rival or the occasional lovestruck miss who might follow him about.

The moonlight silvered the window on the opposite side of the narrow street . . . and then a cloud passed over the moon and the glass darkened. Thomas's eyes widened. "Fiona, come here. I can see quite clearly into the house across the street. I believe that is a bedroom . . . and your neighbor is beautiful. Who is she?"

Fiona crossed the room to stand near him and looked out. "I don't know. She is visiting. The owners of the house are away."

"Is she all alone then?"

Fiona shrugged, a little annoyed by his interest. "I suppose so. I have never talked to her, Thomas."

He laughed softly. "Then it will not seem so wrong to spy on a perfect stranger."

"Hmm. I would rather not argue that point. But if you insist. . . ."

Moving closer, they looked out the window together and Thomas put his arms around Fiona's waist as the woman in the house opposite began to disrobe. She was tall, even when she kicked off her shoes, with a willowy figure and firm breasts. The candelabra she had set by the bed illumined her body but kept her face mostly in shadow.

The night was warm and she sprawled on the bed, leaving the candles burning. She stretched, luxuriating in her nakedness, and opened her legs to reveal an intimate glimpse of female flesh that shone wetly in the candlelight. Then the woman slid her hands down over her belly, sinking several fingers into the dark hair between her legs.

"Ah," Thomas murmured. "I hope that she doesn't stop."

She seemed restless, twisting her hips this way and that, keeping her fingers in her cunny.

"She is imagining a lover," Fiona murmured back.

They watched the woman withdraw her hands and get up on all fours, rearranging the bed pillows into a high mound. She flung herself into them face down, lifting up her hips to tuck a soft little bolster covered in pale velvet between her upper thighs. This she began to squeeze in a regular rhythm, keeping it clasped between her thighs. Her hips thrust down into the pillows, going faster and faster.

The shadows of the candlelight flickered upon the walls of the room they viewed. Thomas gasped. The woman moved with sensual abandon, relishing her solitary pleasure, quite unaware that she was being watched.

Fiona stirred in Thomas's arms. Hugely erect, he drew her tightly against his body as he riveted his eyes upon the darkened window across the street.

What man would not be aroused, Fiona thought with an inward smile, watching a round, womanly arse like that tighten and relax . . . tighten and relax . . . as its possessor enjoyed a private session of frottage, using soft pillows to rub and pump herself to a strong climax. One did not always need a man.

But luckily Fiona had a lover at hand to ease her own restless desire. Shamelessly asking for his attention, she lifted her skirts once more and pushed her bare bottom against the cock that strained against the confinement of Thomas's breeches.

He reached around to grab her cunny with one strong hand. "Ah, good girl. Right where I want you, hot and ready for me."

Fiona laughed softly. "Yes. Always."

"Show me," he whispered. "Play with your nipples while I

penetrate you with your dress up. You know I love to see your arse bared for me. And bare your breasts too. Now."

She obliged, pulling out one creamy breast and then the other, tugging at her own nipples, while Thomas glanced down over her shoulder to see and then returned his gaze at the other woman, still thrusting sensually against the mound of pillows.

Then the woman reared up, reached between her legs and pulled the bolster out. Fiona could just see the wet spot on the pale velvet before the woman flung the bolster on the floor. She lay down upon her bed again and began to stroke and stimulate her cunny, giving it a few smacks for good measure, writhing like a woman possessed.

They continued to observe, fascinated and expecting her to climax at any second. But the woman sank into the pillows, scattered now upon the bed, resting.

Thomas pulled back a little and undid his breeches, taking out his stiff cock and letting it rest upon Fiona's bare behind. She stepped so that her legs were farther apart, granting him full access, although the difference in their height made intercourse in this position impossible.

He hooked a foot over the leg of a low ottoman and dragged it to them. Fiona stepped upon it, holding onto the windowsill with one hand and keeping her gathered skirts up with the other.

The woman in the room opposite rose from the bed and went to the mirror, holding her breasts in her hands. She pinched her nipples hard and repeatedly.

"Do that to yourself," Thomas said into Fiona's ear. She felt the throbbing head of his cock enter her nether lips, but he did not thrust in. "Now. And do it as she does. Pull on your nipples and make them stand out. You have beautiful high nipples, Fiona. I could suck them all night." He clasped her hips and her bunched-up skirts at the same time, giving her a free hand.

Fiona tugged one sensitive nipple, then the other, crying out softly when the feeling intensified, wanting only to make it more intense. Nipple teasing went right to her cunt, and her lover knew it.

"Ah," Thomas murmured. "I love watching two big-breasted beauties play with their nipples. Keep on. It excites me tremendously." He nudged Fiona's swollen cunny with the tip of his cock again, still holding on to her hips. "Which one of you will come first?"

"If all you give me is the hot tip, then I will be crazy with desire. Must I wait? She will come first, mark my words," Fiona said, wriggling back and trying to make him slide inside her. But Thomas was far stronger and held her still.

"I want to make you wait, love. Does it excite you to watch in this way?"

"Yes," Fiona whispered.

The woman turned from the mirror and went back to the bed, rummaging through the drawers of the nightstand. She took out a huge dildo of ivory, with attached balls made of softer stuff, round and heavy, which swayed in the air when she gave them a playful slap.

"Ah. Now for some devilish good play." Thomas's voice roughened with male lust.

Then the woman settled back on the bed and spread her legs more widely than before, touching each bottom bedpost with an elegantly arched foot. Fiona and Thomas had an excellent view, despite the flickering of the candles next to the bed.

They watched her slide the ivory rod in and out, vigorously thrusting it into her snug pussy, obviously enjoying the bounce of the stuffed leather balls against her arse cheeks. Then, without further ado, she twisted up and around, turning her bum to them and holding in the false penis. The sudden screwing motion seemed to excite her even more.

The woman crouched on her knees, reaching back between

her thighs to slide the thing in even deeper, but the last inch or so of the thick, gleaming ivory rod stuck out from her swollen nether lips.

"I would love nothing more than to see you push that dildo in for her," Thomas said into Fiona's ear.

"We must be content to watch," Fiona replied. She heard Thomas gasp when the woman began to rock on all fours, making the dangling balls swing and slap hard upon her cunny.

He could stand it no longer. He rammed his cock into Fiona, all the way. She thrust back against him, matching his strokes, employing the same rhythm as the woman they watched, to give him even more stimulation.

Then . . . they both stopped when a door opened in the room of the house across the street and a tall, well-built man entered, quite naked.

"Perhaps he was watching her as well from the closet or the next room," Thomas said softly, holding Fiona still once more but growing even larger inside her.

Fiona nodded. The woman, half-crazy with pleasure, didn't even notice that she was no longer alone. Her face, when they could glimpse it, was wet with sweat, close to the ultimate satisfaction she craved, giving herself deep, repeated thrusts of the dildo and harder slaps from the attached balls, her mouth open in a moan.

Fiona could see that the woman's eyes were closed, until she felt the man who had entered her room caress her cheek. She raised her head, eyes wide to see his enormous erection was only an inch away from her panting lips.

Thomas began to slide in and out of Fiona's pussy again, with tantalizing slowness but he speeded up when he saw the woman take the other man's cock into her mouth and begin to suck greedily, as if it were the most delicious thing on earth.

Unattended, the ivory rod fell out, pulled down by the heavy balls. The man took his cock from her mouth, withdrawing slowly as the woman tightened her full lips around him, reluctant to let him go. Her lover or master or whoever he was grabbed the ivory one to replace his, putting it in her mouth and making her taste her own juices. The woman licked the long dildo clean, looking up at the man with lascivious affection, eager to arouse him even more.

She succeeded. The man took the dildo away and stroked her tangled hair, her back, her haunches, as if soothing her . . . or preparing her for what he wanted to do next.

Then he turned around, spreading her buttocks wide open and resting his big hands upon them while Fiona and Thomas watched, transfixed. Did he prefer the tightness of the hole that women shared with men? Would he lubricate it with a dash of spit and enter her there? Her beautiful bum was the only part of the woman's body that not been thoroughly stimulated, stroked, or pleasured with a probing finger.

Thomas and Fiona both strained to see, joined and moving in a way that made Thomas bite his lower lip to keep from ejaculating straightaway. "What next?"

"I think I know," Fiona said softly.

The woman kept her arse up but buried her face in the pillows.

"Yes," Fiona breathed. "She loves to play the wanton. And she loves extreme stimulation. He will give her what she craves, Thomas. Just you wait."

"I cannot restrain myself much longer," he growled. "Do keep still!" He clasped Fiona's hips even more tightly. "But do keep talking . . . the sound of your voice is as erotic as the show . . ." He ended with a low moan.

"A man's firm hand upon her soft flesh is what she wants," Fiona went on in a whisper calculated to arouse. "A man who will discipline her but with such gentleness that her resistance melts not from fear but from opening her soul to the one who thus commands her."

As if the man in the opposite room had heard, he curved a strong arm around the waiting woman's hips and gave her a long, sensual, and very thorough spanking with his free hand while she cried out her pleasure and her gratitude for his skill. Then he got on his knees behind her, plunging his very real and thickly satisfying cock into the woman, stroking her sensitized buttocks with especial tenderness to take her to climax at last. The lovers reached the moment at the same second, rocking so closely together that they seemed to be one being, not two, and collapsed upon the bed, twined around each other, lost in erotic bliss.

"Thomas . . . oh, Thomas . . ."

He groaned and rammed his cock into Fiona to the hilt, moving too fast to administer the slaps and tingling smacks she enjoyed so much herself, focused entirely on the irresistible sensation that engulfed his body. Then, with another shuddering groan, he began to shoot pulsing jets of come inside her. "I cannot hold back . . . ohhh . . . my sweet love . . . take it all! All!" He finished with a roar and let her go, stumbling a little.

Fiona hardly cared. She would rather finish herself and remember the erotic scene they had happened to see after he had gone. Though Thomas had done his best, the subsiding organ he was wiping off at the moment was of little use to her. No, she would have a more intense climax with her own hand and her own imagination.

There came a soft knock upon the door. Fiona and Thomas hurriedly put their clothes to rights and turned away from the window.

"Who is that?"

"Sukey, no doubt. With the water for my bath."

"Oh, of course. I quite forgot."

"She has excellent timing." Fiona smothered a giggle. "Just go, darling."

Thomas cast a look at the closed door when Sukey knocked

upon it again, hastily did up his breeches, threw his dark coat over his shoulders without bothering to put his arms in the sleeves, then picked up his boots.

"The footman will assist you with those." Fiona smiled indulgently. Thomas's dark curls and flushed cheeks gave him the look of a lad lately come from a first assignation. Yet he was only a few years younger than she, and nearly as experienced in the myriad pleasures that awaited lovers behind closed doors.

He smiled boyishly. Damn it all. If she was not careful, she might very well fall—

Never, she told herself. *Not with him*. In any case, Lady Fiona Gilberte did not believe in love and had never experienced that unnerving emotion.

"Give my regards to your beautiful neighbor if you should happen to see her on the street."

"I shall do nothing of the kind."

Thomas laughed. "Of course not. Good night, my dearest." He clutched his boots while he gave her one last kiss, nipping her lower lip with the gentleness of a man whose passion had been fully satisfied.

"Good night, Thomas," she said softly.

A clanking and sloshing sound came from the hall outside her door as the unseen servant set a bucket of water down heavily and gave a rather theatrical groan.

"I will leave by the other door," said Thomas. "Though I should like to see Sukey scrub your creamy skin. The little minx must enjoy attending you, Fiona. Tell me, have you two ever—"

"Do shut up," Fiona whispered. She waved to him, one hand on the doorknob so her maid could not come into her bedchamber too soon. He blew her a kiss and closed the other door behind him with a faint click and went down the back stairs. Lady Fiona counted to five, opened the door and looked out to see . . . a large, nearly full bucket standing in a puddle of water. But there was no sign of Sukey.

The puddle of water, nice and hot, seeped quickly into one of her silk slippers. Fie! Was she supposed to lift the damned bucket herself?

Fiona would not. Indeed, she could not. She peered into the corridor and saw Sukey at the other end, talking to the footman, Summers, who usually helped Thomas with his boots. The fellow had one hand on the little maid's round rump and the other was sliding between the front folds of her gown to feel her breasts. As usual, Sukey seized every opportunity to find someone who would appreciate her charms.

"Sukey!"

The maid whirled around before the footman had a chance to let go of the front of her gown. Her breasts popped out, pink-tipped and plump and startlingly white in the half-light of the hall. The footman gasped out an apology, whether to the maid or to her, Fiona could not tell.

Sukey drew the edges of her opened gown together, in no very great hurry to do so.

Fiona only shrugged. She was well aware that the wanton maid thought nothing of displaying her body, having been encouraged to do so by her lecherous master—Fiona's late and unlamented husband—who had been so kind as to seduce the new girl at once and get her with child in the first year of her employment at Aldrich Hall. Sukey had given the unfortunate infant, a boy, to Coram Foundling Hospital on the day of its birth and never spoke of it again.

But Fiona had kept her on nonetheless, feeling that Sukey would be unlikely to disapprove of her mistress's own affairs. A prudish innocent might whisper to the housekeeper and other servants. Therefore, Sukey was permitted a degree of familiarity that Fiona would not countenance from the rest of the staff.

The maid was well paid—and allowed to choose from milady's discarded dresses and inconsequential jewelry from milady's discarded lovers. Were she not bribed in this fashion, Sukey might take it into her head to carry tales to the London scandal sheets, as Fiona knew.

She looked at the footman, who stood up even straighter, his dignity preserved by the rapid decrease in size of a magnificent erection still somewhat visible under his tight breeches. Her late husband had hired only servants with the proportions of classical statuary, liking to watch them rut and romp from various peepholes that he'd had drilled into every secret place in the vast Mayfair house.

At first Bertie had invited Fiona, his newly wedded third wife, to join him in this pastime; but she had politely declined. Her explanation: it was quite impossible to sound properly authoritative to servants she would see naked, whether or not they would know it.

Her elderly husband had not seemed to mind her refusal, since he had married her chiefly for her decorative qualities anyway. And he had cared not a whit that she was no longer a virgin, and had never asked her for particulars on that score.

A good thing, too. She would have hated to explain, with the customary tears and tragic protestations of ruined innocence, that he simply wasn't the first man who'd bedded her. Or the second. Or even the third.

She had married Bertie for his money, not having a penny to call her own despite her impeccable bloodlines. Fiona's father, the impoverished son of a venerable earl who was never going to die, had made the match—and as good as sold his only daughter, she often thought.

This particular footman, Summers, had been hired just before Bertie's death and perhaps had not known of his master's voyeurism. But Fiona imagined he might well prove a satisfying stud. He seemed to be trying not to look at Sukey as the maid sauntered down the hall to her mistress.

"Come. Prepare my bath," she said impatiently. "The water is precisely the right temperature. And do not look at me like that. Such impertinence."

Sukey tossed her head and gave Fiona an insolent look before bending down to the bucket's handle. She hoisted it with ease and brought it through the doorway without spilling a drop, kicking the door shut behind her like a performing pony.

She lugged the bucket through the bedchamber into a connecting alcove, where a gleaming tub stood on lion's paws of bronze. There she lifted the bucket high and poured in the hot water all in one go, a crystalline stream that splashed into the cold water already in the bathtub, sparkling in the candlelight. Steam rose from the tub in delicate wisps.

"Shall I undress you, my lady?" Sukey inquired, looking as if she knew perfectly well that someone already had, at least half way. The rumpled state of her mistress's black velvet gown—the disheveled bed, which looked very much as if someone had been clawing at the covers while in the throes of bliss—gave the evening's delights away.

Of course, the maid knew nothing of the lovers in the house across the street . . . Fiona caught a knowing glance from Sukey. Hmm. Perhaps the girl *had* she seen the show. "There is no need for that, I can manage. Just go."

Sukey nodded and took her leave, swinging the empty bucket by her side and closing the door quietly enough behind her. Fiona heard the maid's footsteps echo down the hall and return, then patter down the stairs. Evidently the easily aroused Summers had decamped. Fiona had no doubt that Sukey hoped to finish what she'd started.

If she didn't waylay Summers, the maid would have to find another man to tease. It was a miracle that Sukey got any work done at all.

Fiona undid the ties of her bodice and let the black velvet

gown fall into a heap on the floor, stepping out of it. Since Thomas had already done away with her drawers, she was quite naked, not having bothered with stays.

She pushed the dress aside with one foot and walked to the alcove, enjoying the feel of the cool night air on her heated skin, wearing nothing but the triple strand of pearls. The rim of the bathtub was wide, warmed by the water within, and there she perched, swishing a hand to and fro through the water, anticipating the delicious sensation of a good long soak.

She touched a hand to her tender nether lips, still slick from Thomas's spunk, wondering if it might be a better idea to wash there first, separately, and deciding that it would.

There was a porcelain ewer and a matching basin resting upon an ebony table in the alcove. Fiona rose, picking up the ewer and dipping it into the tub. She poured the water into the basin and added a soft cloth, wringing it out to just the right juiciness before rubbing it luxuriously between her legs, cleaning herself as thoroughly as a cat.

Stimulating her already far too stimulated flesh in this fashion aroused her once more. She dropped the washcloth back into the basin and stood before the mirror, legs apart, admiring her proud breasts and curving hips for a few seconds. Then Fiona took the little bud that just showed between her nether lips with her forefinger and thumb and stroked it. With womanly delicacy, she increased the speed of her strokes until she felt soft thrills pulse through her body. Fiona closed her eyes, dropping her head back and letting the deeply sensual feeling overtake her.

It was her third climax of the night and much stronger than the two that Thomas had given her before they watched the passionate encounter across the street. A solo session could be extremely enjoyable, she thought dreamily. Of course, she couldn't very well spank herself or kiss her own flesh or writhe the way she liked to in the powerful grip of masculine hands.

Nonetheless, entirely satisfied, she turned once more to her bath and stepped in, settling into the warm water with a blissful sigh. Fiona watched the candles flicker through half–closed eyes, not thinking of anything at all. Relaxed and happy and delighted to be alone, she lolled in the water until it grew cold.

A draft was coming from the bedroom. Perhaps Sukey had left a window open. Fiona shivered and sat up, reaching for a towel and patting the wet pearls that encircled her neck, then rubbing her breasts and arms somewhat dry.

She gripped the rim of the tub and rose from the still water, dripping and looking about for her new robe. Ah. There it was, on a nearby hook. Its silken folds shimmered in the candlelight, and its elaborate embroidery of full-blown peonies and butterflies seemed to glow. Hardly a practical garment, but then Lady Fiona owned very few garments that fit that description.

Her wardrobe was designed to be alluring. Workaday woolens and puritanical linens were not fabrics that interested her in the slightest. She preferred sheer things, soft things against her sensitive skin. And if her dress and underthings could be easily removed by her lover du jour, so much the better. Being attended by a lady's maid before and after an amorous interlude had definite drawbacks. Though Sukey, a little hussy if ever there was one, never seemed shocked by anything.

Fiona clambered out of the bathtub rather awkwardly. Well, no one could be a picture of elegance all the time, she thought, not when faced with the peril of falling on a slippery surface and landing on one's backside with a loud splat.

She tossed the towel with which she had dried her neck onto the floor, and picked up another, wrapping it around her hips and rubbing her bottom slowly and sensually. If Thomas were watching, he would have had her on her knees immediately, her head down and her hands reaching over her hips to spread fully open for him.

He loved to look at her that way, loved to stretch her cunny a bit wider to see the luscious pink of its inside walls before he began the two-fingered fucking she liked so much. Then, before she could have his thick cock, he would give her the royal treatment: prolonged, deeply erotic foreplay followed by delicious bare-bottom disclipine that combined mastery and gentleness. Exactly what the nameless lovers in the house across the street had enjoyed together. Fiona had relished the unexpected show. Very much.

She melted with pleasure when Thomas spanked her that way, not caring if her buttocks quivered under his welcome chastisement—a quivering she could not control and did not want to control, because she knew that the sight aroused him beyond measure.

And she loved the feeling of shameful pleasure that pulsed through her, loved hiding her face in her tumbled hair, a woman with no name and no identity for a little while, begging with her whole body and a few gasped-out words to be dominated by him.

Then, when he could restrain himself no longer, he would ram his hot shaft inside her all the way, until she screamed his name and came hard, thrusting her hips back, back, back . . . taking every drop of his hot come as he too cried out with lusty joy.

Tucking the towel between her legs, she squeezed and then let it drop, reaching for another to dry her legs with quick strokes before slipping into her gorgeous robe. The mirror cast back a reflection that pleased her and she turned this way and that, enjoying the glorious colors and the way it felt to be swathed in expensive China silk.

Her bed had been turned down and a warming pan placed between the sheets, she saw as she entered the room. Had Sukey come and gone so quietly? Yes, her black velvet dress had been picked up by unseen hands and put away. Fiona realized that she must have dozed a little in her bath, but no matter.

How pleasant to simply curl up in a welcoming bed and drift into dreams without further ado.

She bent over the bed, taking out the warming pan and setting it to one side. Then Fiona slipped her robe down her shoulders, enjoying it for a few seconds more before putting it over the chair that stood by the bed.

Quite naked, she slid between the warmed sheets and pulled the swan's-down comforter up to her chin. Heaven. And she was content to be alone. She would sleep well tonight.

2

The morning sun cast a bright ray across her pillow. Lady Fiona wondered drowsily how it had got through the draperies and turned her head away. The room filled suddenly with light and Fiona opened her eyes all the way and rolled back over. Sukey was pulling the heavy brocade draperies apart and singing softly under her breath.

"You are happy today, Su." Fiona yawned.

The maid gave her a cheeky grin. "I have Summers to thank for that, milady."

Fiona laughed and sat up, pulling the comforter up over her bare breasts. "Have you no shame?"

Sukey only shrugged. "Does he, mistress? Did he not pull open my dress and show my tits to you last night?"

"Yes, but he did not mean to—"

"All the same, he thought he might be sacked."

"Dear me, no. Not for that. I knew it was an accident—was it, Sukey?"

"More or less."

"Equivocal words. I suppose I ought to reprimand you. But as long as no one knows, I don't really care."

Sukey moved about the room, putting things to right, and letting in the tweeny when she knocked. The younger girl, a new servant hired by the housekeeper, came in with a tray laden with a tea service and something freshly baked hiding under a napkin that covered the silver basket.

"There is someone belowstairs to see you, milady." The girl bobbed a clumsy curtsey after she set down the tray.

"What? It is far too early for social calls."

"It is past noon." Sukey said.

"Oh, dear. I suppose I must arise."

"Who is it then?" Sukey asked the tweeny.

"She said her name was Mrs. Mellon, I think. That tall man, Mr. Henchley, spoke to her. He seems to be in charge of many things."

"Yes," said Sukey rather rudely. "He is the butler. Very full of himself, he is. Likes to give orders. Not that I listen."

Fiona sighed. "Oh, dear. You ought to, you know. If only for the sake of appearances." She smiled at the tweeny. "Mrs. Mellon is my cousin, but only by marriage. And she is my dear friend."

The tweeny nodded.

"I do not receive callers in my bedroom as a rule," Fiona went on, "but she has seen me *en deshabille* before. Sukey will show her up."

"Yes, milady." The tweeny bobbed another curtsey, as if she were practicing. Sukey turned the girl around and propelled her out the door, following immediately behind and shutting the door firmly.

Fiona threw back the covers, and stood up and stretched. A visit from Harriet Mellon required preparation, as the woman was an incessant—though entertaining—chatterbox who might dally for an hour or more. First things first: Fiona dashed into the watercloset next to the alcove, straddled the bowl and pissed, rising after several seconds with a pleasant feeling of relief. She wetted a washcloth and dashed it between her legs. Well and good. It was not as if anyone was going to sniff there.

Then she came back into the bedroom, still quite naked and lifted a corner of the napkin covering the silver basket on the tea tray to see what was beneath. Scones. Excellent. And was there jam? There was. Perhaps she could cram in a few mouthfuls before Harriet reached the bedroom and began to talk.

She broke a scone into pieces, slathered one with jam and butter, and nibbled it, pouring a hasty cup of tea and downing that next. The sound of slow footsteps reached her ears. No doubt Harriet, who was plump, was carrying Beastie, her pop–eyed spaniel, to save the spoiled dog the trouble of climbing the stairs.

Fiona reached for her silk robe upon the chair where she had left it last night, slipping it on and tying the sash firmly about her waist. She ran a brush through her sleep-tangled hair, putting it up with a few hairpins, glad she'd had a thorough bath the night before. A glance in the mirror told her that she looked presentable.

The bedroom betrayed no trace of a man's presence, she noted with a look about into the corners. Of course, Harriet undoubtedly assumed that Fiona had a lover.

Because I always do, Fiona thought smugly. Not that one had ever mattered much more to her than another. Charming as Thomas was, it was variety that she liked more than anything else. And if all of London wanted to whisper about her, as Harriet had often hinted, let them.

Of course, dear Harriet was inquisitive to a fault. She might very well try to winkle information on the subject out of Fiona. But there was no need to name names. The simplest thing to do was get Harriet talking about her own sexual adventures, as these were often disastrous—or comical.

Her cousin's husband served as captain on merchant ships to China, bringing back tea and fine porcelain and all manner of odd knickknacks to please his amorous wife. The Chinese were unsurpassed when it came to erotic carving, and Harriet had a remarkable collection of ivory penises, larger than life, some with testicles, some without.

One, Harriet's favorite, a foot-long specimen with enormous bollocks, had been ingeniously fitted with a tube through the tip and a small rubber reservoir at its base that required only a slight jab from a finger to simulate the male climax.

Ned had told his wife that the thing was used to teach the fine art of fellatio to novice prostitutes—and also used to excite men who liked to watch women suck a dildo while they had a real cock jammed inside them too. And, according to him, other whores sometimes joined the fun—for an additional fee, of course—reaching from behind to tickle the happy customer's balls as he banged away. A hard poke or two and the dildo spurted thick white sugar-water, a treat to lick up at the high point of excitement. Cries of joy all around, a few swipes with a towel, a hasty refill of the dildo, and the next man would enter the chamber of decadent pleasures for another go.

Perhaps her cousin had some new toy to show, Fiona thought with a smile. She heard Harriet arrive upon the landing and traverse the carpet that led to the door of her bedchamber. The spaniel made a gasping noise, but from the lack of a thump, Fiona assumed that it was still clutched to its mistress's bosom. No doubt it wanted to get down, if only to preserve a few shreds of doggy dignity.

"There, there, my poor Beastie," Harriet trilled. "I have you safe and sound. But you ought not to wheeze. You are not the one who has been climbing these damned stairs." She stopped outside the door and knocked. "Fiona? Are you decent?"

"Yes, Harriet." Fiona flung open the door with a welcoming smile. "How delightful to see you and Beastie!"

The spaniel let its tongue loll out and gave Fiona a pop-eyed stare while it wriggled in its mistress's arms. Harriet held onto it, as well as a bulging reticule that was emitting a mysterious soft chime.

"What is that noise, Harriet?"

"Oh, that is my latest present—or presents, I should say, from Ned. Really quite amusing. I brought a set to give you, but all in good time. Good morning, Fiona!" She bustled in.

"Will you join me for breakfast? There are scones."

"Oh, Beastie hates scones. Have you any bacon?"

"No."

Harriet kissed the spaniel on its moist black nose. "Alas. No bacon, my love. But you will survive." She set Beastie down, and he waddled over to an ottoman and squeezed himself underneath it, panting rapidly.

"I daresay he will," Fiona said, putting her arm through her cousin's and drawing her into the room and toward a capacious armchair. "Would you like tea, Harriet?"

"Oh, yes. I find I am extremely thirsty. Your house has far too many stairs. And too many rooms. How you must rattle about here now that you are a widow. Don't you get lonely, Fiona?"

A leading question if ever Fiona had heard one. She smiled politely. "Not at all."

"Then perhaps you have recovered from the shock of dear Bertie's untimely death."

"Bertrand drank himself into an early grave," Fiona said matter-of-factly. "The doctor said his liver was as hard as rock. He had turned a most unattractive shade of yellow towards the end and the lowest whore would not touch him. You know as well as I do that he got his hand up every skirt that he could. I do not miss him."

Harriet nodded. "He was not a saint, certainly." She settled herself into the armchair with a sigh and investigated the tea tray, lifting up the napkin and poking at the still warm scones. She broke off a piece just as Fiona had done, put twice as much butter and jam on it, and ate it daintily. Then she poured out tea for both of them.

Fiona helped herself to another scone, sitting on the edge of her bed and devouring it with greedy pleasure. Never mind the crumbs. Eating in bed was yet another good thing about not having a man around the house to quibble over such things. Harriet handed Fiona a cup of tea and drank her own, her bright blue eyes sparkling as she looked over the thin rim, sipping through pouted lips.

The word for Harriet, Fiona thought absently, was . . . succulent. Her round body was not the height of fashion but there seemed to be no shortage of lust-crazed gentlemen ready to bury themselves in her sweet flesh when her husband was at sea.

Fiona finished her tea and glanced discreetly at the clock. Five minutes had passed between the setting down of Beastie and the taking of nourishment. Refreshed and strengthened, Harriet was sure to launch into a tale of her latest conquest within seconds. And Fiona was curious as to what was in the bag that her cousin had set upon the floor.

The clock ticked softly in the quiet room. The spaniel wheezed and then snored. Harriet set down her empty cup and swept the crumbs from her lap, looking at Fiona's attire. "What a magnificent robe. The material is Chinese, is it not? The embroidery is very fine—wherever did you get it?"

"I believe it is an Oriental design. The robe itself is my dressmaker's handiwork."

"Dear Fiona, I assumed as much. One cannot simply buy such things in shops. It is splendid. You look like . . . an empress."

"I am not sure that is a compliment."

"Oh, but it is. The color suits you, my dear cousin. Or do

you have a new love? Who's put that lovely pink in your cheeks, eh?" Harriet laughed heartily.

Fiona swung a leg back and forth rather impatiently and made no answer to that question.

"I quite approve," Harriet continued. "You must not mourn forever. You are young and may marry again."

Fiona raised an eyebrow. *Marriage? Fie. Perish the thought.* She still dressed mostly in black, of course, because she looked good in it. She had mourned her late husband for exactly the period of time that society prescribed, and not a minute longer.

Harriet did not seem to notice that her cousin wasn't saying a word. "So you sleep in pearls, do you? You are a lazy cat, Fiona." She squinted at the triple strand, which Fiona had forgotten that she still wore. "Or perhaps a sentimental one. Were they a gift?"

"Yes." Not that Fiona would confess who the giver was. She reached up and turned them around so the clasp was in the back again.

Harriet cleared her throat. "Hmm," she said slyly. "I think I recognize the clasp. From Coburn's Jewellery, is it not? All the married gentlemen shop there. But not with their wives. And not for their wives. Not that I am one to talk," she giggled. "Dear Ned never asks what I am up to while he is gone."

"And you don't know what he's up to, either. He probably has a wench of every color in every port."

"No doubt," Harriet said affably. "In any case, those pearls are very pretty, Fiona. Now, do tell me who gave them to you."

Fiona drew the flat lapels of her robe high up around her neck. "No. There is no reason for you to know."

Harriet looked hurt. "But we share every confidence, my dear cousin. I tell *you* everything. I know that I may speak to you with perfect frankness, on every subject under the sun and that you will never judge me or tittle-tattle."

Fiona knew that the best thing to do was distract Harriet,

which was never difficult. "I am glad that you think so. Now, what do you have in that bag?"

Harriet looked down at the bulging reticule she had set on the floor and gave it a little kick with a silk–shod foot. Whatever was inside chimed softly once more.

"They are Celestial Spheres—have you not heard of them?"

Fiona shook her head. Harriet reached down and picked up the bag, drawing apart the strings that closed it and taking out two smooth balls of ivory, as big as eggs but perfectly round. She rolled them back and forth in her palm, making their cleverly hidden mechanism chime as they struck each other. Fiona looked more closely. She could see no seam in the ivory where the halves of each sphere had been fitted together.

"Ned said that the Chinese give these toys to their women, as it is impossible to keep all of their wives and concubines sexually satisfied."

"Ah."

Harriet nodded and let the balls roll in her cupped palm again. "He showed me exactly how to use them."

"Hmm. Then he *does* have other women."

"What of it?" Harriet said nonchalantly. "But he is very good to me, Fiona, when he is in London."

Fiona laughed. "So long as you are both happy. Now explain the Celestial Spheres, if you please."

"The woman lies on her back, with her hips raised on a soft silk pillow. She puts the balls deep inside her pink blossom—Ned says the Chinese have many names for that—and rocks her hips so that they move and make her love petals wet with dew."

"I see."

"He gave me a little book with pictures of a concubine demonstrating their use."

"Thoughtful of him," Fiona said.

"You can see the ivory balls within her since she seems to have no hair there—well, I have the book, Fiona." She patted the reticule and smiled. "The pictures on the fifth page are delightfully lewd. Two younger concubines hold the lady's thighs apart and put the balls in, then make her clasp her pink blossom with open fingers. They help her bounce her pretty bum up and down on the pillow while a third one licks between the lady's fingers, dainty as you please, and she has her climax with all of them watching. The Celestial Spheres are supposed to give great pleasure."

"And do they?" Fiona inquired. She looked at the balls in her friend's hand, wondering how they would feel inside her.

Harriet shrugged. "I have not tried my set as yet, even though Ned has been home for an entire week. He brought me several sets, in different sizes, for my toy chest, as he calls it. I shall try them, you may be sure. He likes to see me enjoy his presents, especially if I put one toy in my cunny and another in my arse."

"Both at once?"

"Sometimes." Harriet didn't even blush. "He always wants to spread my arse cheeks first—he loves it that I am so big and soft behind, Fiona." She wriggled that part of herself against the seat cushion of the armchair and continued. "He begs very nicely for the honor of putting in a small dildo, if that is my pleasure. I have him put a dab of French cream there to ease the way."

"Of course."

Harriet sighed happily. "Just talking about arseholes makes him so hard."

"That's a sailor for you," Fiona murmured.

"Well, yes. If he is very good, I bend over and let him touch the tight puckers with a fingertip and rub in the cream but no more. It excites him exceedingly. He knows I know it."

"Go on," Fiona said, quite amused. There was no stopping Harriet once she began to talk about sex. "What next?"

"I part my cunny lips and slide a huge rod inside, all the way up. Ned is mad for such play, especially when I finally ask him to gently stimulate my arsehole with the little rod I prefer there—watching his dear wife experience penetration fore and aft is his greatest desire, he says. Sometimes the sight makes him come without my even touching him."

Fiona shook her head, reaching out to take the spheres from Harriet's hand. "And do you moan long and low? Such a show requires appropriate music."

"Indeed I do," Harriet laughed. "Ned says he could find me in the darkest whorehouse just by the noise I make."

Fiona could think of no reply to that. Harriet most certainly did speak frankly about every subject under the sun. "Well, well. Thank you for the spheres, Harriet. Are they the largest of the sets you have?"

"Yes. I put these aside especially for you, my dear friend. Of course I prefer the real thing, Fiona."

"As do I. Still, these are interesting. And the sound they make is very pleasant."

Now that Fiona was playing with the spheres, Harriet had her hands free to look inside the reticule on her lap once more. "The book—ah, here it is. I will leave it with you." She handed it to Fiona with a wink. "Do you understand Chinese?"

"You know perfectly well that I don't."

"Then enjoy the pictures, as I did."

Fiona riffled through the small volume. "The secrets of the East are revealed at last. It seems that they enjoy the act of love as we do." She stopped at one page and turned the book sideways, then upside down, to study it. "Good heavens. However did they manage to get into that position? One would have to be an acrobat, which I am not. But thank you, Harriet. I will peruse it later."

Harriet clucked to her spaniel and they both watched Beastie wiggle out from under the ottoman, then jump into her ample lap. "Perhaps your new friend will enjoy the pictures as well. What did you say his name was, Fiona?"

"I didn't say."

3

As the day continued fine, Lady Fiona decided to ride out in Hyde Park after Harriet's departure. From the open carriage that she drove herself, she looked down upon the crowd jostling each other in the leafy paths and edging by their superiors, whose numbers were far fewer.

The breeze puffed out the dresses of the promenading ladies, whose sedate pace did not alter no matter how high their hems were lifted. It was as good a way as any to permit the gentlemen a glimpse of pretty shoes and stockings that would otherwise be hidden, Fiona thought.

Women had to do what was necessary to capture masculine attention if they had ensnared no likely prospects for matrimony by late spring. The season was well underway and the bachelors of the *ton* would soon be departing for their country estates, to spend the languorous months of summer in pursuit of trout and the more willing servant girls of the household.

Yet the married women seemed as eager to catch the eye of the men who strolled by, sometimes alone and sometimes in groups of two or three. Some men rode, putting on a display of muscular buttocks in breeches that were almost indecently tight, their thighs gripping the saddle leather in a most provocative way as they trotted by on the finest horseflesh in London. From behind she could glimpse something even more delicious: the balls of the well-endowed men, compressed slightly by the supple buckskin that contained them, but very much there. Fiona never tired of that sight.

She would not have minded being swept away by such a man for a wild ride over a moonlit moor, if a convenient moor could be found that was not too cold or too desolate, she thought with an inward smile. He would clasp her to his chest with one strong arm during their desperate ride . . . his stiff cock pressing into her bouncing behind while she clung to the saddle horn and rode astride, just as he did.

Fiona let her mind drift and elaborated upon her fantasy of ravishment. He would know that her soft cunny smacked the saddle with each bounce and that would make him grit his teeth and groan with hot longing . . . until, wild with desire, her faceless lover would make the horse rear and scream, then dismount to lay her down upon the heather . . . well no, that was scratchy stuff. Anyway, he would make her come again and again.

The very thought made her feel randy. It was rather at odds with the decorous scene through which she was driving at the moment, certainly, but the fleeting fantasy was quite diverting.

Fiona did not see the piece of paper that the breeze tossed under her horse's nose, but she felt a hard jerk as the animal shied and the reins went flying. Both her hands clung to the side of the carriage when the horse launched into an all–out gallop that sent the strolling fashionables scurrying to safety on every side.

Fiona had not the breath to scream. The horse swung away and headed over the greensward as the shouts receded. She heard only the dull thud of pounding hooves and the rattle of the light carriage. It was likely to lose a wheel at this breakneck pace over open ground or shake itself to bits with her in it. But there was nothing she could do besides hang on.

Another sound came to her ears, of faster hooves overtaking them. One of the horsemen upon the Hyde Park paths had come to her rescue, an excellent rider who brought his mount near as he dared to her panicked animal and made a swift grab for the loose reins.

He missed. He grabbed again and missed again. Then, whether from the closeness of the other horse or simply because hers had grown tired, the hooves slowed to a trot, and then, blessedly, a walk. The winded gelding finally stopped . . . and hung his weary head.

"As well you might," the man said softly. His voice was deep and soothing. He reached for the reins as he halted his mount and got them at last.

"Th–thank you," Fiona stammered when she found the strength to speak. She put a hand to her forehead, shielding her eyes from the strong sun. Her bonnet had been lost in the pell–mell gallop and her hair had come unpinned, tumbling down over her neck and shoulders in waves of glossy honey. "That was a trick worthy of the Roman arena. Do you race chariots, sir?"

Her rescuer kept both sets of reins in his hands as he dismounted. "No. But I was a cavalry officer, and I and my horse are veterans of the Peninsula battles. You might say that we learned that trick together."

He made soothing noises to her gelding and stroked the animal's sweating neck with fine, strong hands turned a deep color by a foreign sun. Despite that, they were a gentleman's hands, she thought, wishing that he would stroke away her trembling as well.

He dropped the reins, moving to her carriage to help her down. She alighted upon the grass, almost too weak to stand, but she stiffened her spine and took several deep breaths, then felt a little better. They were not far from the shade of the trees, where she might sit and rest. Then Fiona realized that she would have been thrown instantly from the carriage had her runaway horse swerved to avoid the trees, and began to tremble again.

The man noticed. He slipped off his light riding coat and put it over her shoulders, saying only, "Wear this. And do not argue."

She looked up at him with astonishment. "Why would I argue?"

He smiled slightly. "A riding coat does not go with an elegant gown, milady."

"I don't care. It is comforting. And it smells very nicely of bay rum, and—" *And you*, she wanted to say, but didn't. A powerful, virile man who had ridden hard and risked his neck to save her. "What is your name, sir?"

"Edward Finch, Lord Delamar, at your service."

"I am—"

"Ah, but I already know who you are. The Incomparable Fiona. The Belle of Mayfair. Also known as Lady Gilberte. The young widow of that filthy old scoundrel who died under mysterious circumstances. You are as lovely as the scandal sheets say. But did you poison him, as they also say?"

"Wh–what?" she sputtered.

He was opening a small compartment at the back of her carriage and seemed not to notice her consternation. "Do you have a lead rope? Ah, here is one. We can tie the horses while you rest and tell me everything."

She felt inclined to fling his coat to the ground and tread upon it. Yet he did not seem to be the sort of man who would be intimidated by a fit of womanly pique. "There is nothing to tell," she said at last.

"Of course not. I was speaking in jest, but I apologize. You are still upset, understandably so."

Fiona looked back at the distant path to the point where her horse had bolted; the crowd that had fled before her had resumed their peaceful promenade. Then she looked back at him.

He offered no more explanation of his remarks about the scandal that had sullied her reputation—what little remained of it, she thought—and was busying himself with the horses and leading them a little distance away once he had freed hers from the tangled harness.

He returned. "Since you have not asked for my forgiveness, Lord Delamar, I shall not give it. But I accept your apology." There was a noticeable edge in her voice.

He nodded, giving her the slightest of smiles. "Rest assured that I never believe what appears in print. The scandal sheets provide coarse entertainment for the rabble, nothing more."

"Ah, yes. They were out in force upon the path. Did some low fellow notice me and mention my name?"

"No." He smiled. "I was riding close behind you with a friend. A very respectable friend. But he knew who you were."

"I see. And when my horse shied, did he tell you to come after me?"

Lord Delamar shook his head. "When I saw the danger you were in, I spurred my horse and came on straightaway. I don't suppose that my friend or the others thought you had lost the reins; only that you had decided to amuse yourself with a mad dash. You have a reputation for being rather wild, you know."

"This conversation seems to be going in circles. You have returned to the subject of my reputation, such as it is."

"So we have," he said genially. "Well, if it is any comfort, we are two of a kind. I am not received in the very best drawing rooms myself."

Lady Fiona favored that unexpected response with a slight smile of her own. "Is that why your friend did not follow you? I suppose that being seen with you is bad enough, but adding a scandalous female like me is far worse."

He snorted. "I have very little use for propriety, milady."

Fiona pondered that interesting statement as she walked up and down. "Then I am glad that we met, even under these circumstances."

"Yes. Wild horses brought us together. It seems quite fitting, does it not? We are as far from polite society as one can get on a sunny afternoon in London. Do you have a blanket?"

"I beg your pardon?"

Lord Delamar rummaged in the compartment where he had found the lead rope. "Let me see. Ah—here is a very fine blanket. It smells strongly of horse but that can't be helped." He shook it out and picked a few bits of dry grass from its rough wool.

She was amused by his carefulness and watched without comment as he bent down to pull the corners into neat right angles. Military training, of course, she thought with a smile. That Lord Delamar had been an officer did not surprise her.

That he bore a startling resemblance to the amorous highwayman she had imagined did.

His thighs were as hard, his body as powerful. And his features were a striking improvement upon her faceless fantasy. Lord Delamar was handsome, with a long scar upon one cheek that only made him more attractive. The scar cut through a deep dimple that flashed when he smiled and added an ironic twist to his expression that intrigued her.

"Madame." He made a gallant wave at the blanket. "Please sit down. You need not fear grass stains upon your beautiful arse."

"My wha—you are impudent, sir." Her tone was properly indignant, but secretly his candor secretly amused her. If he wished to waste no time furthering their acquaintance, she was in agreement. Just looking at his long, strong legs, braced apart as he stood with his hands on his hips, and the breadth of his chest was enough to make a fool out of any woman.

"That light gown hides very little, Lady Fiona. The sight of you in it would tempt the devil himself."

"I wore it because the day is warm. And I did not know I would meet the devil upon a Hyde Park path today. Or that he was so handsome."

Lord Delamar grinned wickedly. "Thank you."

She stepped onto the blanket, sinking gracefully down into her skirts and letting his coat slide from her shoulders. She kicked off her shoes and tucked her feet under the folds of the airy muslin, looking about to see if anyone was nearby or watching from a little distance.

They were quite alone.

Edward settled down beside her, stretched out on one side and rested his head upon his elbow. His eyes moved over her with slow pleasure, taking in every detail of her body, from her rounded thighs to her high bosom but lingering longest upon her face. It was quite clear that he liked everything he saw.

She returned his scrutiny but more discreetly as he took off the neck tie that had come undone during his chase and tossed it onto the blanket. The loose linen shirt he wore hinted at the brawn beneath, and his buckskins hinted at nothing but showed everything. His natural endowments were quite evident in that close-cut article of clothing. Soft leather covered a long hard cock and balls that would fill her palm with satisfying heft.

She looked up and caught him watching her. He laughed in a devilish way and rolled over on his back. "So, my lady—where shall we begin?"

Fiona folded her hands primly in her lap. "Not here, my lord." Had they been anywhere but out in the open, she would have undone his breeches and freed his sex from its confinement. She was eager to see it jut out, ready to be stroked and sucked; eager to tease his scrotum with gentle fingertips until it tightened over his balls, eager to watch him ejaculate in healthy spurts and hear him groan with lust when he did. But . . . not here.

"Oh? My dear Lady Gilberte, the look in your eyes tells me—"

"I have told you nothing, merely made small talk."

"Then continue to talk to me, Fiona," Edward said. "There is no harm in that, surely. You have a very pleasant voice. Soft and sultry. Like summer rain."

"Hmph."

"You seem displeased by the compliment."

"Did you expect me to blush and giggle?" she asked tartly. His flattery had pleased her nonetheless. And a pleasant chat in the dappled shade was a decorous way to begin an affair—she had no doubt that they both had the same thing in mind.

There was no reason to be discreet about it.

Although the promenading crowds were far away, her wild ride and Lord Delamar's pursuit must have been thoroughly discussed and dissected by now, and certainly all assumed Lady Fiona had spurred her horse into dashing away so she could lead him on.

None of which was remotely true—she hadn't known he was behind her or even who he was until he introduced himself. Fiona had heard something of Lord Delamar, of course, though she rarely paid much attention to gossip, having been the subject of it so often.

She let her gaze drift over his long body, enjoying the sight of so fine a man so close to her. So he likes to hear women talk, she thought. Then he is easy to please and even easier to seduce.

It would not be long before she had him exactly where she wanted him: in her bed.

Three weeks later . . .

Frowning, Lady Fiona dipped the nib of her quill in a bronze inkwell and added another line to the morning entry in her diary. *Lord Delamar remains frustratingly out of reach.* She sketched his profile in the margin with a few deft strokes.

Damn the man. Thoughts of him filled her every waking hour and he even hovered in her dreams.

Since their first meeting, Edward had commandeered more space upon the pages of her diary than any of the other lovers chronicled in it, except that she had not one word to say about his sexual prowess, inclinations, or appetite.

She had no real reason to complain, since Thomas was constant in his devotion and called upon her twice a week. But compared to Lord Delamar, Thomas seemed . . . callow.

Edward stopped by now and then, never staying long but always unfailingly polite. Fiona was dismayed by her eagerness to see him, as she ran downstairs when she heard Henchley let him in, thrilled by the sound of his voice exchanging a few pleasantries with the butler, excited beyond measure simply by seeing him standing in the gloomy marble hall of her Mayfair house, looking warm and virile and so very male.

Surely he ought to make the first move, declare the desire that she knew she saw in his eyes, throw her down upon the nearest sofa and have his wicked way with her . . . but no. He seemed more interested in her opinions of the latest plays, Whitehall politics, the weather—talk. Talk, talk, talk. *She* was sick of it, no matter how much he might like the sound of her voice. In fact, she was ready to scream with frustration.

She would have to take the lead, she supposed. Invite him to dinner with a few others for the brilliant conversation he desired, feed him lightly and ply him with a judicious amount of wine . . . but too much of either and he would be of no use to her. Then, once the other guests had decamped, she would take him by the hand and *drag* him to her bedroom if necessary.

If only he would seize an earlier opportunity—and her beautiful arse, as he had called it—and do what they both wanted to do! She had no idea why he held back.

Perhaps it was just as well at the moment. With the extra servants hired on to ready the Mayfair mansion for the household's summer exodus to the country, there was not a private moment to be found, let alone a private space.

Fortunately, the army of servants had already attacked the dining room, first rubbing every crystal on the chandelier until the monstrous thing positively sparkled and then polishing the long table until the fine wood glowed. The carpets had been taken up, taken outside, and whacked nearly to bits to rid them of dust. All was in readiness in that one room at least.

But what to have for dinner? Fiona twiddled her quill in her fingers. She swore under her breath, realizing that she'd dotted her morning dress with ink as a result. She rose and struggled out of it, then ran out of the library in her chemise and drawers, calling for Sukey and throwing the balled-up dress down the stairwell when the maid replied faintly from the first floor.

"Sukey! Have Eliza wash this at once! The ink might come out—perhaps not. But she must try!"

Feeling very cross, Fiona stamped up the stairs to her bedroom to find another dress, planning the courses for the dinner party as she went.

Aspic of something. *Stamp*. Cold roast chicken. *Stamp*. Salad of field greens. *Stamp*. Summer puddings and sorbets. *Stamp, stamp, stamp*.

The upper landing was blessedly free of bustling servants, and she dashed to her bedchamber before any appeared. From the next room, Fiona heard the swish of feather dusters and the heavy groan of furniture that was rarely moved. It would be draped in white canvas while the cleaning was done, giving the room a ghostly look.

The entire house seemed to be inhabited by diligent ghosts, as the servants swathed themselves in enormous aprons and moved through it. The yearly cleaning was nothing new but it made Fiona feel altogether unsettled and her unfulfilled longings for Edward Finch, Lord Delamar, only made matters worse.

Fiona was not the only one at sixes and sevens. Sukey had been in a foul mood after giving up on Summers, the footman who'd ripped her dress. Fiona got the whole story from the housekeeper, Mrs. Geffrye, a handsome and capable West Country woman who did not mince words. She'd said Summers had plenty of willing wenches eager to drop their drawers for a hard pounding and a teasing little bitch like Sukey must have seemed like too much trouble.

And so the maid had recently turned to another man, though he was not on the Gilberte staff and no one knew who he was. Certainly Sukey spent far too much time primping and preening of late—Fiona had caught her at it more than once but had not scolded her. She assumed that her maid's new lover was someone's valet—servants seldom dallied with anyone below their own station in a household.

At least Sukey had someone. Lady Fiona dipped her pen once more and added a final thought. *But I shall have my way—milord shall dine with me on Friday next.*

She opened the drawer that contained her stationery and sealing wax and took out several sheets of paper. It would be no easy task to compose an invitation that hit precisely the right lighthearted note and held a hint of seduction as well. A faint smile curved her lips. Certainly Lord Delamar was the sort of man who could read between the lines . . . if he wanted to.

Fiona had found out much more since their chance meeting in Hyde Park: he was a notorious rake, never wed, breathtakingly rich, and capable of pleasuring a woman all night long. None had ever succeeded in capturing his heart. All of which only intensified her desire for him.

4

The dinner went well enough, as disasters went. The courses were brought forth on platters, served up by solemn servants under Henchley's watchful eye, the food pushed about with forks and knives but not eaten. *Did everyone truly think that she had poisoned her late husband after all?* Fiona wondered. She frowned when the platters were lifted from the table and taken away, but no one seemed inclined to take another bite.

Of course, the most distinguished of the invited guests had declined to come, sending last-minute regrets on crested stationery, and the company was far from brilliant.

Besides Lord Delamar and Fiona, there was Harriet, filling the lengthy gaps in what passed for conversation with cheerful prattle, and Captain Ned Mellon, who sank his chin into his starched collar and scarcely spoke. Harriet's rich aunt and her harrumphing husband, in London for what remained of the season, had condescended to attend as well but seemed unwilling to waste words on any other topic but their money and what it could buy.

Worst of all, Harriet had seen fit to bring Beastie, who snuffled under the table in a fruitless hunt for crumbs. When the spaniel gave the rich aunt's ankle an inquisitive lick, she shrieked exactly once and then fell silent, glaring at Harriet.

"Dear aunt, do not look at me like that. It is not as if *I* licked your ankle," Harriet said sensibly.

"I wouldn't put it past you," the aunt retorted, watching the progress of the dog as he walked to the other end of the table. Beastie bumped out the tablecloth as he went, while circling other ankles and causing the guests to sit up straighter.

And a good thing, too, Fiona thought. The gathered company had seemed to slump as the evening wore on—with the exception of Lord Delamar, whose upright posture was as perfect as everything else about him.

She sighed inwardly. With a little luck her guests might all leave soon, save him. She supposed she could plead a headache, but then Lord Delamar might take it as a reason to leave as well.

Captain Mellon yawned and mumbled something about the lateness of the hour. Harriet took the hint and winked at Fiona, as if she guessed that her cousin wanted to be alone with Lord Delamar. Perhaps Harriet, whose airy chatter concealed her shrewdness, knew that the gathering was a ruse.

Had she not once called Fiona a cat—and a lazy cat at that? No doubt Harriet understood that the formal dinner had been nothing more than a way to get a wary man within pouncing distance.

The rich aunt rose stiffly, took one more look around in case the unseen ankle-licker was about to spring, and left the dining room, her husband in tow.

The women made a beeline for their wraps and reticules, allowing the men to assist them as Sukey was nowhere to be found. Fiona would have to scold her lady's maid for inattentiveness later, but for now she watched Beastie, unrepentant, bring up the rear of the parade to the hall, waddling and gulping.

She said goodbye to the group with a prodigious sense of relief. Alone at last. Lord Delamar had bid the other guests adieu as they all rose from the table and he'd gone into the drawing room, followed by Henchley with the port and savories.

Fiona waited until she heard the carriages roll up and then away. She looked toward the drawing room as the butler exited with the empty tray and held the door open for his mistress.

"Thank you, Henchley, that will be all." He nodded and walked away. Lady Fiona smoothed her dress and stepped into the room. There was Lord Delamar, making himself comfortable in the biggest armchair, sipping her best port. His legs were apart and stretched out, with one foot propped on an ottoman and one upon the floor. He sat up when he saw her, a gentleman once more, which she regretted.

"Thank you for a delightful dinner, my dear lady," he said.

"You are welcome, milord." There—that took care of the formalities. Would it be very wanton of her to simply jump into his lap and kiss him senseless? She did not want to scare him but she had no wish to wait another moment when she had been waiting for nearly a month as it was.

Lord Delamar set down his glass as he rose and walked to where she was standing. "Excellent port."

"Thank you."

"Henchley brought in a more ladylike drink as well." He nodded at a bottle of champagne, chilling in a crystal bowl filled with cracked ice. Fiona wondered where the butler had procured that precious stuff—the ice, not the champagne—at the onset of summer. Henchley was indeed a treasure.

"I was wondering—after you have refreshed yourself, of course—if we might walk through the house together. I have heard that it is full of wonderful things, thanks to your late husband. He was reputed to be a great lover of beauty in all its myriad forms."

He clasped his hands behind his back and looked down upon her with that faintly wicked grin. Fiona did not reply at once. Bertie, the old roué, had been much gossiped about and she wondered what Lord Delamar knew about her husband—and why he wanted to know more. "Yes, well, he bought paintings and statues by the shipload," she said at last. "And there are no end of family portraits in this house. If you are interested in art, there is much to see."

Should she begin with the oil portraits of Bertie's exceedingly proper ancestors . . . and save the scandalous erotic engravings hidden away in leatherbound folios for last?

Fiona decided against the ancestors. The grim faces of generations past would be enough to intimidate any man. But why had he asked to tour the collection? Lord Delamar's bland expression gave her no clue as to what he might really have in mind. She rather doubted that he was all that interested in art. Certainly he had given no indication of it during their frustratingly polite conversations in the past weeks, although he always listened to her raptly.

She knew that he loved to listen . . . but she would soon be yowling like a cat in heat if listening was all he did.

Perhaps *he* was waiting to pounce on *her*. A straightforward, skirts-up, breeches down, rump-pumping session on the divan as he sucked her tits and fucked her front, back, sideways, inside out, and upside down would be a start, damn it all. But she was piqued by his ability to keep his distance and his polite composure irritated her immensely. Was there no way to shatter it?

Fiona thought for a moment longer, studying her quarry as he studied her. What did he want from her? More importantly, what did she want from him?

There would be no answer to either question until she had provoked his passions somehow. Now that she had him where she wanted him—feeling the mellow glow of the best port in her cellar and giving her smoldering looks—she was still not sure what to do.

How did one seduce a notorious seducer? Perhaps being demure was best. No skirts up. No breeches down. Just her leading him on through the halls of her Mayfair mansion, come what may. Henchley would have to warn the servants to disappear.

She looked up again at Lord Delamar, admiring the breadth of his shoulders and chest, and the warm male scent that emanated from him. His immaculate linen and tightly cut buckskins had been chosen to show off his physique, of that she had no doubt. Oh, how dearly she wanted to be the cause of a visible erection under the soft leather of his breeches, wanted to stroke the hard ridge of it while she whispered in his ear. . . .

Fiona made up her mind. If he liked the sound of her voice that much, then perhaps talking would be an excellent way to begin the seduction. Scheherazade had entertained a sultan with a thousand and one tales; but Fiona might tempt milord with just a few.

Her only problem was where to begin. She had listened often enough to Bertie describe the frenzied couplings of the servants—and not a few of the houseguests—he had spied on, just as she and Thomas had spied on the couple in the house across the street.

Fiona felt a slight pang at the thought of her lover. He had taken the edge off, so to speak, while she had been secretly fantasizing about Lord Delamar. But two days ago she had seen Thomas assist a music hall dancer into a waiting carriage after a matinee performance and drop a furtive kiss upon the woman's freckled bosom. No doubt Thomas was kissing every damned freckle on the tits of Miss Tra-La-La Tippytoes by now, especially since Fiona had not invited him tonight.

Well and good. Perhaps it was best if their affair ended amicably. She'd amused herself with him but nothing lasted forever. The here and now was more important. And here was Lord Delamar, tall and virile and—waiting for her to make the first move.

He cleared his throat as if trying to get her attention. "Where shall we begin, my lady?"

"That is a question you have asked me before."

"Have I?"

"Yes. In Hyde Park, on the day we met."

"Ah, yes. I remember. You didn't really answer."

Fiona gave him an arch look. "Is that not a woman's privilege?"

He inclined his head in a polite nod, but there was a fire in his dark eyes that excited her.

"I suppose the answer is . . . tonight, milord. And we might as well begin right here."

"If you wish." He made her a formal bow, at which she turned away, frustrated once more but he added a lascivious wink at the last second.

"Did you say there was champagne?" she inquired.

Somewhat later . . .

Fiona was happily riding upon one of Edward's thighs, her soft arms wound around his neck, feeling giddy. They had shared a bottle of cold champagne. She pressed a kiss upon the muscular column of his neck, running a hand over the fine linen of his shirt and teasing his small male nipples with little brushes of her fingertips. Edward sighed with evident pleasure—until her exploration was interrupted by a light knock upon the drawing room door.

"That is Henchley," she said softly into Edward's ear.

"I suppose we should spring apart."

"No need. He will not seem to see. He is very good at that." As the butler opened the door and looked in, Fiona looked up from her perch on his lordship's knee and gave Henchley a mischievous smile. She knew he would respond with bland correctness, as if the man in whose lap she sat was invisible.

"Milady." He gave a slight bow. "Will you require anything else?"

"No, Henchley." She raised an eyebrow as she spoke, a sufficient signal to a man her late husband had trained to be discreet. The butler gave her an infinitesimal nod in return.

Lord Delamar tossed back the rest of his port. Henchley entered the room to retrieve the plates and whatnot, filled his tray, and withdrew almost noiselessly.

She tousled the hair of her handsome guest, not quite ready to rise from his lap. "As I was saying, I thought we might start with the Red Room. Bertie had it done in scarlet silk to show off the paintings he bought on his last trip to Italy."

"I am a great admirer of the Italian masters."

She nodded. These particular Italian masters had been great admirers of the female form. And many of their models had been painted with nothing but gossamer over their flawless breasts, hands touching their pubes, hiding nothing despite the glorious hair that cascaded from their heads in rivers of auburn and gold. The sensual effect was much more erotic than frank nudity and one could well imagine what had gone on the moment the painter had set down his brush. Viewing Renaissance nudes should be an elegant stimulant for a gentleman of Lord Delamar's caliber.

"Tiepolo? Titian? Whom do you prefer?" She nuzzled his neck just under his ear, stroking the trace of stubble along his jaw. No doubt his valet had shaved him close, but the hour was late and Lord Delamar had a very attractive slight shadow by now.

"That is a difficult choice to make. Is the sun more beautiful than the moon? I could not say." He extended his arm and she slipped hers through it at the elbow, well pleased to walk so close to his side. There was an ease in his tone that took nothing away from the powerful masculinity she sensed lay beneath his excellent manners.

Still feeling the heady effects of the port and champagne, Edward and Fiona left the drawing room and headed down the hall together. He looked about, seeming to make a mental note of everything he saw, she thought without wondering why. Simply being this close to him was affecting her ability to think.

They had passed several carved doors when he drew her close. She felt a shiver of animal joy in the warmth of his embrace, exulting in their aloneness. Anything might happen. They were, however, some distance from the nearest bedroom.

"Where are we going, Fiona? One might easily be lost for days in a mansion of this size," he teased.

"Oh, we did come upon the odd wanderer now and then," she giggled. "A husband looking for a straying wife, and vice versa. Especially after parties. Bertie put up signs to misdirect guests and ensure that everyone had as much fun as possible."

"I see," Lord Delamar said. "So there is truth to the rumors about this house and your late husband."

"Indeed there is," Fiona replied cheerfully. "But he preferred watching to doing. He never tired of observing others at it. Come this way. We can go into the Red Room later." She brought him into a small alcove and let go of his arm to open the doors. "You might call this his observatory, in fact."

She gave him a smile that was anything but demure, intending to speed her planned seduction along. There was no point in holding back, or acting with missish reserve. Their brief dalliance after dinner—complete with ardent kisses, caresses, and her boldly riding his thighs—had been a promising start. Even Henchley's interruption had been welcome, since they were now only one flight of stairs away from her bedchamber.

There would be a few amusing detours on the way, of course. Like this one.

Plain furniture of dark, gleaming wood was just visible in the moonlight that came in through the undraped windows, which looked out onto the blank back wall of another wing. A desk and some chairs had been set upon a thick carpet that muffled their footfalls as they crossed the room.

"Did he use a telescope?" Edward asked. "There is nothing to see from this window but bricks."

Fiona smiled. "There are peepholes. He had them put into the walls of certain rooms. I will show you one."

She searched for the right panel and found it after a minute, sliding it back to reveal not one but two small peepholes, with fisheye lenses rimmed in brass, about a yard apart. Edward looked at them curiously. "Ah. Most ingenious. A lens that gave him a full view but prevented the people in the room from seeing or hearing him."

"He kept silent as he watched, I assure you. He very much enjoyed listening to the sounds of passionate lovemaking, especially when the participants had no idea they had an audience."

Edward raised an eyebrow. "Indeed."

"Did I shock you?"

"No." His voice was quite controlled.

But Fiona did not give up that readily. "Oh dear. But I wanted to shock you. I am feeling positively brazen, my lord. It might be the champagne . . . or it might be your presence."

"I am flattered. I think." He clasped his hands behind his back and stood with his legs apart.

Fiona looked down at his crotch ever so discreetly, then up at his wolfish grin. "Shall I tell you why there are two peepholes?"

He paused a moment before replying. "Yes."

"Bertie liked company."

He gave her a wry glance. "And did you join him, Fiona?"

"Not as a rule. But go on—have a look." She clasped his upper arms and propelled him forth, laughing at his resistance.

Edward went along with her playfulness and she moved her hands down, sliding her arms around his waist from the back as he put his eye to the peephole. "I see a bed. A four–poster, square and solid, like the other furniture. It seems to be a man's room, as far as I can make out. But no one's there." He turned around and put himself in front of her, just barely pressing his lower body against hers.

Fiona noted with delight that the slight contact was arousing him once more. "Shall I tell you what went on in that bed?"

He stroked her face. "Such a sweet smile for a wanton woman. It may prove my undoing. Yes, tell me. Tell me everything."

She looked up at him, wanting to see his expression as she began her tale. "John Tresham had that room. Our former butler, before Henchley."

"Henchley seems the soul of propriety," Edward murmured, brushing a stray lock of her hair back into place.

"Well, Tresham was not. But he gave excellent service. He was a very handsome man with a sensual mouth. Every woman in London who had heard of his skill longed to have her pussy expertly licked by him and quite a few of them did."

Edward drew in a breath. "You *are* feeling brazen. But I like to hear you talk, as well you know." He brought her closer still.

She broke free from his embrace and took a few steps back. "He took care of our girls too. Since he also supervised the staff, they had to finish the chores first, of course. But he treated them with respect and they very much enjoyed their tender reward at the end of the day. Seeing him on his knees, satisfying the maids with just his tongue, was very arousing to watch."

Lord Delamar gave her a considering look. "But you said that you did not watch."

"Ah, but Bertie told me many things, Edward. He used to

say that it was all part of a bride's education. Would you like to know more?"

He drew in a deep breath. "Very well."

Excellent, Fiona thought triumphantly. She could see, thanks to the moonlight that came in through the undraped windows, that the erection she'd provoked only moments ago was getting bigger by the second.

How nice to know that he found her voice so alluring. But Fiona thought it best to stay a little distance away from him for now—if only to be able to observe his intensifying arousal, hear his breath quicken, see the front of his breeches tighten. She glanced down to see how it was coming along.

Very nicely. He was huge. His cock pulsed slightly when he realized where she was looking.

If he should choose to unbutton his breeches and let his aching member spring out—expecting, naturally, that she would offer him the satisfaction of release with her hand or mouth since she had gone to so much trouble to tease him—why, she would make him force it back in and button up his breeches herself. She would allow her hand to rest upon his engorged flesh while she sweetly begged his pardon.

"Continue, Fiona. And you can gaze at me all you wish. It excites me when women do. They pretend not to see what men have but they like to look on the sly." He took a chair and faced her, letting his muscular thighs fall open and placing his hands upon them. She feasted upon the sight: he was bull–big, equipped to please women who craved complete fulfillment.

"Indeed. We are very good at sizing men up."

"Yes." His voice was rough and low. "Keep talking to me, Fiona. I like the game you are playing, even if you seem to be making up the rules as you go along."

Lady Fiona watched him move one hand to the front of his breeches and adjust the hot, stiff flesh trapped within. Ah, if he were naked and doing that . . . just the thought of him encircling his shaft with strong fingers and cupping his balls at the same time excited her. A cock that fine deserved to be caressed by her much smaller hand—oiled first, perhaps, then stroked to an explosive orgasm.

She realized that Edward could see his reflection in the mirror from where he was sitting and so could she. How incredibly sensual it would be to give him the pleasure of seeing himself at the moment of climax, watching hot spurts of come drench his hand as he squeezed just under the heavy, plum-purple tip—no, she was rushing things. Fiona wondered whether she should sit or stand to finish her first tale.

The husky, masculine vibration of his voice, though he had spoken only a little, had made her exceedingly restless. Fiona decided to pace.

"As I was saying, Tresham supervised our maids and rewarded the good girls—"

"What about the bad girls?" Edward smiled slightly. "Forgive my interruption. Go on, Fiona. Your soft voice excites me more than I can say."

"Very well. If that is your pleasure, then it is mine." She let her gaze fall once more on the front of his breeches. "The butler made them wait their turn, even when the wenches were ready to tear out each other's hair to advance in line. There was more than one cat fight during Tresham's term of employment."

"You are exaggerating. Surely he did not have women lined up on the stairs outside his bedroom. He would not have had time to sleep."

"I am repeating what Bertie told me."

Even with that reassurance, Edward looked a little dubious. "Of course. Well, pray continue."

"Our Tresham preferred the new maids, just come from the country."

"Did he initiate them?"

"Yes. Some had never even touched themselves. The shyest pulled their long skirts over their faces when they lay back upon his bed."

"Ah," Edward said softly. "Keeping their drawers on?"

Fiona nodded. "Some kept their boots on as well. But they all came to him of their own will, anxious to experience what their bedmates in the garret whispered about."

She paced faster, excited herself. "A new maid would let Tresham kiss and caress her cunny through the cloth first . . . and then let him open the split in the middle. Next he would touch her private parts just so, spreading open the inner lips for the pleasure to come, and teach her to find her little bud and play with it. He licked there so skillfully that she would reach orgasm within a minute or two, just like all the others. Tresham was able to relieve their nervousness and pent–up desire with ease, and he was always very gentle. They returned to his bed again and again."

"Back to the bad girls, if you please."

Fiona looked at him and smiled, knowing that the giddiness of the champagne had worn off and been replaced by a joyous sexual excitement. She could say whatever she pleased. "They liked rougher play and he made sure they got it. Tresham had them crouch over his face, and let them bounce their bums up and down, burying his face between their cheeks with each bounce. He particularly enjoyed licking a juicy cunt while fondling a fine big arse. The more experienced wenches would reach forward for his cock, and stroke it with hands made strong by housework until he groaned and spurted all over his belly. They were never shy at getting each deep thrust of his tongue."

Edward put his arms behind his head and got comfortable in his chair, tipping his pelvis up slightly. The action made his cock seem even larger. It was all Fiona could do not to raise her dress and straddle him.

It would be easy enough to have an orgasm just pressing against a rod like that, her thighs spread wide open as she rocked in his lap . . . especially if he held her in his big hands and squeezed her buttocks, kissing her all the while.

As if a similar thought was running through his mind, Edward gave her a heavy–lidded look in return. "Come here, Fiona."

She obeyed, but still kept a little distance, unsure of herself and of him. With lightning speed, he reached out and clasped her wrist. "Lift your dress, my lady. Show me your juicy cunny. You can turn your face away like the shy maids in your story if you like. But let me look my fill. I like to look just as much as you do."

As if he knew she would not refuse, he let go of her wrist. Fiona hesitated, then bent down to pick up the hem of her dress. She wasted no time pulling her dress up high on her thighs and then to her waist, standing before him in drawers of muslin so fine it was almost sheer. Lord Delamar patted the nest of springy curls that showed through the front, and bent his head to press a kiss there. Then he parted the split in her drawers with one hand, holding it open with the other and touched a big finger to her tender flesh. "You are already wet."

He stroked her sensitive bud next, still using just his fingertip and she drew in her breath with a gasp. He had gone right to it, not fumbled or poked as so many men did, and her cunny throbbed in response.

"Sweet lady," he said softly. "Spread your hidden lips open for me. I want to have my fingers inside you and watch your face at the same time. How many fingers do you like? Two? Three?"

"Two," she whispered, sliding a hand over her cunny and doing as he asked. "Your hands are quite large."

He slid in two fingers with care and Fiona clutched her dress, swaying a little on her feet. She was tight but slick and the slow penetration felt wonderful.

"What a tempting picture you painted for me, Fiona. Pretty maids all in a row with their dresses up . . . and their most private parts fully exposed. A handsome manservant kneels to give each what she craves . . . that was a nice touch. He licks and licks . . . and they moan . . . just as you are doing now."

She had not realized that she was moaning. Edward was thrusting his fingers in and out, still keeping it slow.

His single-minded concentration upon her arousal was having the desired effect. She wanted to simply push her hot pussy into his face but even sitting down he was too tall for that. He looked at her intently and stopped thrusting, leaving his fingers inside her, using the pad of his thumb to stimulate the throbbing bud above.

With a little cry, Fiona got a better grip on her bunched-up skirts and parted the front of her drawers so quickly that she ripped the seam.

The slight sound made him look down. He slid his hand out of her cunt and pushed the muslin back with the other hand, fully revealing her cunny. He stroked her hips and sides. "So you are ready to tear your clothes off—good. I like seeing you standing so demurely in front of me—with your dress up and your drawers ripped . . . wanting sexual attention that you are not quite bold enough to ask for."

"But—" she began to protest. She had not meant to tear her drawers, which were still fastened at the waist anyway, and she certainly considered herself bold—*oh*.

Edward kneeled before her and applied his tongue to her private parts, giving her a gentle and thorough licking, treating her most sensitive flesh almost worshipfully. But he avoided her clitoris, wriggle as she might to put it in the way of his tender tongue. She clasped his head to her body and stroked his hair, abandoning herself to this exquisite intimacy.

He pulled back and wiped his mouth on his sleeve, smiling up at her. "What a feast. You are delicious, Fiona."

"Ohh . . . must you stop?" The erotic sensations began to ebb—but she wanted them never to end. "Please," she whispered. "Satisfy me."

"I think," he said softly, clasping her torn drawers at the waist, "it is time these came off." With a forceful tug, he split the center seam all the way through to the waistband and yanked her drawers down to her ankles, leaving her bare below the waist save for her white stockings and shirred garters trimmed with satin rosebuds.

"Oh!"

"Keep your dress up, Fiona. Let me look at you this way." His voice lowered to a growl. "Half-naked . . . a little embarrassed . . . and very excited. Turn around."

"I cannot—not with my damned drawers around my ankles—and my shoes have come off!"

Edward smoothed a hand over her hip and began to tease her cunny with the other. "Well, you don't need to turn around. I can see your beautiful behind in the mirror from here. Two perfect globes . . . and so white."

She looked over her shoulder. Indeed, he had positioned himself—and her—just right. With her dress up and her drawers in a tangle that she couldn't escape, her bare legs and bottom were bathed in the moonlight that filled the room and reflected off the mirror. Edward's hands slid over her hips and gripped her firmly. "Bend over. Rest on my shoulder. I want to know if I can see your cunt that way."

Swept away by excitement and the heat of the moment, she did as he asked, supported well enough by his strong shoulder and steadied by the hands that cupped her bottom. The pressure of their bodies kept her bunched dress up around her waist the way he wanted it but the lowcut bodice let her breasts pop out. She tried to pull it up again but could not quite grasp the cloth. "I am falling out of my damned dress!"

He gave her arse a friendly spank and kept her where she

was. "Your clothes are falling apart. How convenient. You can play with your lovely breasts while I play with you."

"How do you know they are pretty?" she retorted. "You cannot see them if I am thrown over your shoulder."

He gave her another spank, a little harder than the first. "There are many advantages to being tall. I have been looking down your bodice most of the evening."

Fiona squirmed and he clasped her tightly around the thighs with powerful arms. She knew he was watching her in the mirror.

"Ah . . . do that again, Fiona. Your sweet pussy shows when you wriggle in that wanton way. I like it."

Keeping an inescapable grip with one arm, he fondled her there, then gave her several spanks that smarted, distributing them equally between her right and left buttocks. She rose up and twisted free—or tried to, not wanting to admit that submitting to his will excited her.

"When I am ready to let you go, I will. But first, kiss me, Fiona." He slid her down over his chest, letting her nipples brush over his shirt, and covered her mouth with his, sliding his tongue over hers, and luxuriating in the ardor of her response.

He grabbed her bottom and pulled her right against him, kissing her deeply and grinding his cock, still compressed under the supple leather of his breeches but achingly hard, into her belly.

Fiona shuddered with the pleasure of it, on fire from his nearness, his strength, and most of all from his desire. But she struggled free.

5

He let her go with reluctance. "So the rules of the game change again. Why?"

Fiona let her dress fall and smoothed its crumpled folds. She did not know quite how to answer his question. In truth, she was unnerved by the strength of her unguarded response to him. "I like to take my time."

"Oho. Is that why you sat on my lap and kissed me so ardently and told me a wonderfully filthy story? Two can play at teasing, Fiona."

"What do you mean?" she asked breathlessly, feeling foolish now that they were apart. She scarcely knew what to do next now that her clothes were in such disarray and her breasts still half out of her gown. She yanked the bodice up over them.

Edward pushed a drifting lock of her hair back into place with a fingertip. "You have been trying to get me into your bed from the day we met. I knew it from the way you talked to me even then."

Fiona stepped out of her tangled drawers somehow and

kicked them away. "You were unfailingly polite, I must say. Not at all what I expected from a rogue like you."

"Who told you I was a rogue?"

"Everyone knows it."

"Then what did you want from me, Fiona?"

She stopped herself from telling him the truth. *What you just did. And more.* "Never mind," she said at last.

He grinned and tipped up her chin with a finger. "I did not say your methods were ineffective. There we sat, discussing politics and the weather and the health of his Royal Majesty, et cetera, and whether I wanted sugar in my tea. It was all I could do not to take you in my arms and ravish you upon the tea cart. But I did want to know you a little better." He planted a relatively chaste kiss on her lips, just as if nothing had happened between them besides polite conversation.

She fought the impulse to slap him. "Well . . . now that you have had your tongue and fingers in me, I suppose there is little else to discover."

He shook his head. "I look forward to continuing our acquaintance."

Frustrated by his bland reply—not to mention the fact that he had not brought her to climax—and feeling somewhat dazed, Fiona said nothing but looked about for her shoes, which had come off with the tangled drawers she'd kicked aside. She bent over and patted the heap of muslin, taking out one shoe and then the other, and pulling up her dress to put them on. The drawers were a dead loss and she left them on the floor.

"I find I am most interested in what goes on inside your head, Fiona."

"Is that why you are looking at my legs? Surely white stockings do not excite you."

He smiled, placing his hands on his hips. Fiona noticed that he was still hugely erect. "Your legs are lovely."

She slid her feet into the shoes and stamped a little to get the toes to fit, still seething with frustration and the sexual heat he had awakened. "Poxy shoes. I think a heel is broken." Taking that one off, she flung it at the wall. Its mate soon followed.

Edward closed the distance between them and took her in his arms. He held her—just held her—for a long moment and made her ache with longing for him. "Ah, Fiona. You manage to look elegant, even when you are cursing and throwing shoes. Always a lady, eh?"

Hardly. At least not at the moment. She was getting nowhere, no matter what she did, and feeling more confused by the minute. Perhaps she ought to have worn stockings in whorish black and not ladylike white—oh, damn. There was no sorting out her confused feelings. Her perplexed scowl made him smile again.

"Well, here we are, my dear—halfway to heaven. But we seem to be having our first spat."

"Shut up."

He grinned and let her go. "We might begin again. Yes, I think that would be best."

"Oh, do you?" She paced a few steps away and turned her back to him, standing in front of the window. She could not remember Thomas ever making her so angry—and she certainly could not remember wanting him as much as she wanted Lord Delamar.

From behind she heard him walk closer to her. "The moonlight shines through your gown, Fiona. I can see that you are naked underneath."

"That is not news." Her tone softened nonetheless.

"Naked . . . and irresistible."

He stood behind her and caressed her shoulders, dropping a kiss upon one and moving upward to her neck. He nibbled on her earlobe and ran his tongue around the rest of it, reminding her of the very great pleasure he had given her south of her tingling ear. Damn him. The sensation weakened her resolve.

"Perhaps our game got out of hand. But I did think you were enjoying yourself."

"I was," she admitted in a small voice.

"Then you will enjoy what is to come even more. But allow me to propose a few rules, Fiona."

She turned within the circle of his arms and let her hands rest on his shirt front, unfastening his neck cloth but leaving it draped around his neck and beginning on his buttons. She folded the white linen back, admiring his smooth, strong neck and the fine dark hair upon his chest. "Very well."

He gave her a hug. Fiona rubbed herself against him like a cat, unable to resist his sensual warmth. Edward caressed her bare flesh under the light dress appreciatively. "Rule one. I may ask you to lift your dress as you just did, at any time I wish."

"All right. I have done it once, I might as well do it again."

He nodded. "Rule two. You must allow me to lick your cunny again. I enjoyed it and so did you."

"Indeed." She felt an unwilling smile curve her lips. How could she argue?

"Do you agree to rule two?"

"Yes."

He held her closer to him. "Rule three. If I desire to see you bare your breasts and play with your nipples, or if I want you to bend over and spread your cheeks and give me the best possible view of your cunny and arsehole, or if I ask anything at all, you must say yes."

"Anything at all? You will not hurt me, my lord?"

He kissed her on the nose. "Of course not. I just like looking at you. Every inch of you. And I intend to satisfy your every desire as well."

Fiona pondered his words. "That sounds reasonable." She slid her hands down his body and stopped just short of his breeches.

"Now touch me." His voice was low. He pulled his shirt out

and let the loose linen billow out, holding the front of it up to allow her to do just that.

She slipped her hand inside the waistband, pulling it away from his taut, hard belly and peeked inside his breeches. There, less than an inch away, his cock stood proudly, a pearly drop upon its tip. She touched a fingertip to the tiny hole to take up the drop and bring it to her mouth. He watched her tongue tip come out and lick that one precious drop. The ridged muscles of his midsection tightened under skin that was hot to the touch, and his long, stiff cock seemed about to burst out of his breeches.

"Delicious," she said softly.

He drew in a long breath. "There will be more of that for you to taste, if that is what you like in your mouth. Much more." She slid a hand into his breeches again but he grabbed her wrist and prevented her from touching him. "You shall come first, my lady. But there is nothing soft for you to lie on in this room. Can we enter the butler's bedchamber from here?"

"Yes," she said. "This way." He let go of her wrist and intertwined his fingers with hers. Fiona took him through an empty closet with a false back that proved to be another door, slipping her feet back into her shoes along the way.

"Very clever. You must give me the name of Bertie's carpenter."

Fiona sniffed. "The last thing he fashioned for my husband was a coffin. We all wondered if it had a secret exit, you may be sure." She swung the door open into the room Lord Delamar had glimpsed through the lens in the wall and brought him in.

She glanced around. "The bed seems bigger once you are inside the room, doesn't it?"

"Big enough for Mr. Tresham and his happy harem," Edward said with a smirk. He sat down in an armchair to pull off his boots, which he thunked into a corner.

Fiona wasted no time in testing the mattress, which had

been made up with a sheet and flat-stitched comforter, but no drapes hung from the canopy. She kicked off her shoes again before the last of her was on the bed but Edward made a sound of protest. "Oh no. Leave those on." He picked the shoes up from the carpet and pushed her down onto her back without further ado. "Raise your legs."

Laughing, she did, letting her dress fall around her hips, baring herself below the waist as before. She parted her legs suddenly, giving him a mischievous look as she flashed her cunny, then brought her legs together and held them straight up, toes pointed.

He clasped her ankles in one big hand, slipping on the dainty shoes one at a time and running his other hand over her smooth stockings, toying with the garters that held them up just above the knees. Then, in one swift move, he pulled off his loosened neck cloth and used it to tie her ankles together and to the canopy rod above.

"There. Ready to be licked?"

She bent her knees a bit to test her bonds, amused by the speed of his action. "Ahh. Yes. Oh, yes." From the second his tongue had touched the heated flesh between her legs, she had wanted more, wanted to come with his mouth all over her cunny, holding his head and surrendering to his sensual expertise. The thought of abandoning herself utterly to erotic pleasure with only a silken restraint to remind her of who was now master of the game, excited her deeply.

Edward knelt by the side of the bed, pulling her hips toward him until Fiona's arse was off the bed, her back still solidly upon it, and her arms stretched out. Dragged in this way, her dress rose higher still and the bodice forced her breasts out. He rose and fastened his mouth tightly upon one nipple, sucking it deep pink and hard. He kept the sucked nipple between his finger and thumb, rolling it as he sucked the other one.

She arched her back, thrusting her breasts at him, stroking

his hair as he nursed her blissfully for a minute or more. Then he stopped with a sigh, pulled his shirt over his head, and treated her to the sight of his beautifully muscular chest, traced with fine dark hair that tapered into his breeches.

Fiona reached out a hand to the cock that bulged inside, strapped back by the tightness of the leather but responding to her touch.

"May I . . . ?"

He ignored her question and went back to his position on the floor, kissing her naked thighs and bottom all over, wherever he could reach, then stroked her backside. Then he put his mouth upon her cunny, getting his tongue in with darting licks.

With her legs together and trussed up, she was much tighter. His tongue had to thrust hard to gain entrance and he used his fingers to stretch her more open, following fingers with tongue, fingers with tongue, in a deeply erotic rhythm that made her thrash as much as the silk tie would allow, bucking her arse.

"Mmmm." He stopped licking, held her steady, and began to suck her bud. Fiona moaned with pleasure. The sensation was intense—and he made it stronger when he sat back on his haunches, fondling her swollen nether lips between fingers and thumb, pressing them together, looking at her now and then and murmuring gentle encouragement.

"Come for me. Come."

She felt an incandescent desire for release, wanting him to witness her first orgasm with him and wanting to experience it with shameless abandon. Deep within her body waves of pleasure rose and rose, never cresting but only taking her higher.

Then she felt him touch her arsehole, stimulating it gently but not penetrating her there. Fiona rested, needing a moment of tender distraction from the climax that was seconds away. She knew very well that such play would make the ultimate sensation much more powerful—and she trusted him, vulnerable though she was with her arse in midair and her ankles tied.

He must love to see me like this, she thought. He was breathing hard when he kissed and tongued her cunny again, keeping his fingertip circling upon her arsehole, slick with the juices that had dripped down.

"I shall not put my finger in, my lady. But I think you enjoy gentle arse play," he whispered when he lifted his handsome head. He began to stroke her buttocks, moving his fingertips over the backs of her thighs, brushing them so softly that she began to tremble. Her need for release was almost overwhelming.

But Fiona wanted him to give it to her. Her hands were free, yet she would not use them. "I beg of you . . ." she moaned, "Now . . . I am ready . . . now."

He stood up, untying her ankles and let her legs down, rubbing them and ridding them of stiffness. The deep, massaging strokes were soothing and stimulating. He cradled each of her thighs in a strong arm as he rubbed it down, moving to her calves and feet more swiftly, intently aware of the swollen pink cunt that was spread open in front of him, awaiting his pleasure, whatever it would be.

"Please," she whispered one more time. "At least let me take you in my mouth, my lord. I must have you somehow. I must . . ."

He undid his breeches and took them off so quickly it seemed to have happened by magic. His legs were strongly muscled, his buttocks indented as if meant to be clutched by a passionate woman. And then there was his cock, jutting out nine inches or more from his taut groin and a nest of very dark curls. His foreskin was rolled back to reveal a plum–size head, tipped with a few more pearly drops of come that she wanted desperately to taste.

"Let me suck you," she begged. "Let me pleasure you as you have pleasured me."

He shook his head. "We shall pleasure each other, my love.

My mouth on your cunt and your mouth on my cock. Lie back. Stay there."

He climbed onto the bed, proudly and completely naked, and turned around above her. Fiona opened her mouth to receive his member, taking as many inches as she could. But he did not thrust. He held still, letting her suck and stimulate him with her tongue, which she wrapped around his cock this way and that as she kept him in her mouth, devouring him.

"Touch my balls," he said, his voice ragged. She stroked his scrotum, feeling it tighten and draw upwards. "Ah—like that. Yes. Oh, Fiona, yes," he moaned. "Just like that. Good girl. How good it feels . . . oh!" His cock trembled and jerked in her mouth as he began to ejaculate.

Fiona clasped the shaft to keep him from ramming it in but kept the top two inches in her mouth, sucking him hard. He moaned and buried his face in her pussy, attending to her with gentlemanly ardor even as his semen filled her mouth. Discreetly, she spat out the first pulsing shots he fired and swallowed the last of it, loving the way he came, healthy, strong and hot.

Then her own orgasm took her by surprise. His vibrating moans triggered an unbelievably intense wave of sensation as he sucked her clitoris with lascivious tenderness, lapping up her juice the way she lapped up his.

They collapsed side by side, still touching each other intimately, and rested in a tangle of sweaty sheets and one very disheveled gown.

6

Simultaneous climax . . . mutual bliss . . . she could not ask for anything more. Fiona rested her head on Edward's thigh for a minute and gave his private parts an appreciative pat. She rose up on her elbows and looked down at him, lolling in the tangled sheets like a big, sensual, satisfied animal. Fiona smiled. "There is nothing in this room to wash with. Off I go—my own bedroom is not far away.

"Did I not lick you clean?" he murmured. He raised his head an inch or so to look at her. "I seem to remember it was you. Perhaps it was not." Laughing, she threw a pillow at him, which he caught and tucked under his cheek, letting his eyes drift shut. "Thank you, my love."

"Am I your love then?"

"Do you want to be, Fiona?"

"Hmm. I don't know." She moved to the edge of the bed. "Stay here. I'll return shortly."

He yawned. "See that you do. I will be ready for a second round by then." He rolled from his side to his front, lying spreadeagled upon the bed, his muscular buttocks tapering into very long and equally muscular legs, his strong arms flung out upon the sheets.

Quite a tempting presentation of naked male flesh. Alas, it would have to wait until later. But not much later, she thought happily.

Fiona eased off the bed, smoothing her dress and running a hand over her snarled hair. Ah, the perils of passion. It would take her a little while to brush it out. She rose, looking about for her shoes and then remembered that she had thrown them against the wall in the other room. She would have to go back to her bedchamber in stocking feet and hope that no servant saw her.

Sukey would have come and gone, and readied her mistress's bed for the night by this time. It was probably safe to venture forth, but even so, Fiona opened the door to Tresham's old room quietly and peered down the corridor before she left. It would not do to have the household abuzz with gossip, especially at the beginning of what she hoped would be a long and satisfying love affair.

She padded down the hallway, turned right and went past several doors to her bedchamber. There was a faint noise coming from within . . . a rustling . . . a thump . . . and then another thump. Fiona swore under her breath. Sukey must not have finished preparing the room—or someone must be finishing Sukey.

Fiona turned the doorknob and rattled it for good measure. If Sukey was indulging in a dalliance with her new lover, whoever he was, the maid had exactly five seconds to escape his amorous clutches, assist the fellow out the window and down the drainpipe, and resume dusting some object that needed no dusting whatsoever. Fiona counted slowly to five and added an extra three seconds. She flung open the door.

All she saw was Sukey's rump. The maid was bent over inside Fiona's closet, tidying the shoes lined up underneath the dresses and gowns. She backed out, holding a pair of fancywork slippers that Fiona knew the maid had wanted, and looked her mistress up and down. "La! You are a sight, milady. Whatever have you been doing?"

"Oh . . . nothing." Fiona gave the girl a lofty look, hoping to forestall any further inquiries. "You may go. And you can have the slippers."

Still looking surprised but pleased enough with the bribe, Sukey murmured a goodnight and left.

Fiona crossed hastily to the mirror. Her flushed cheeks and messy hair quite gave her away, but even the impudent Sukey would not have mentioned it. Her dress had been twisted a dozen different ways during Edward's lovemaking, and was damp with sweat, still warm from the heat of both their bodies. She pulled it off over her head and, suddenly bare all over except for her stockings, remembered that she'd left her torn drawers in Bertie's observatory, as well as the shoes.

Drat. She would have to dress quickly, drag a brush painfully through her hair—Sukey's fingers were far better at untangling such love knots—and put on a different pair of shoes.

Fiona managed all three in less than five minutes, but she didn't bother to replace the drawers, preferring to go bare beneath. She went into the bathroom, hoisted her skirts and cleaned herself intimately, then soaked a washcloth, wringing it out so it would not drip. She was soon on her way back to Tresham's room, where she supposed that Edward was sleeping the sleep of the gods.

A good snap from a cold washcloth on his bum ought to wake him in a hurry.

She opened the door moments later, delighted to see him sitting up in the pillows, quite naked. His knees were drawn up, revealing a thatch of curling dark hair between his muscular thighs, and his soft member resting on his balls. Edward tossed a pillow or two to the floor, reclining and spreading his thighs to give her an even better view of the beautiful big cock that had filled her mouth.

"Welcome back. I missed you."

"I was not gone long." She unfurled the washcloth and tossed it to him. Edward caught it and rubbed the cloth slowly over his balls, lifting his cock out of the way and then stroking and squeezing it.

With pleasure, Fiona watched him clean himself. There was something natural and unconcerned about the way he did it, and again she was reminded of a sensual animal at ease.

"May I kiss you there?"

"My lady, nothing would give me more pleasure."

She bent forward, making herself comfortable, and took his already stiffening organ into her mouth, licking him tenderly to a full erection within minutes.

Fiona stopped and sat up, loving the sight of him with his thighs apart and the huge cock jutting out from between them, bobbing when she looked at it and rising higher. "Hold it tight. I want you to stroke it," she said, "while I tell you another story."

"Ah. So you are in charge again." He grinned and took himself in hand. "Very well. The further adventures of Tresham, is it?"

"No, someone else."

Edward kept his encircling hand under the head of his cock, giving the shaft long, slow strokes while she watched for a minute.

"Begin."

She touched her fingertips to the underside of his balls, rubbing him there gently as he continued to stroke himself. "We had a laundress, Shelagh, a tall, strapping woman with red hair who was as good-looking as she was strong. Our coachman, Danny, was smitten with her."

"And did they meet in this room as well?"

Fiona smiled. "No."

"Let me guess. The stables, then. He bent her over a hay bale and fucked her silly."

She shook her head. "They met in her room belowstairs. She used to work half-naked because of the steam in the room from the boiling wash and all that."

Edward, who had paused, resumed his slow stroking. "How naked is half-naked?"

"She wore only a chemise and drawers. Then one day Danny came in to fetch a clean collar because my husband was going riding in Hyde Park with his mistress and Bertie wished his man to look respectable. The room was hotter than usual and Danny saw that she had taken off her chemise. Shelagh was ironing. Her breasts were large, and they bounced and swayed as she slammed the iron down and slid it over the damp shirt upon the board. Danny was mesmerized. He watched in silence but she did not see him for some time."

He looked at her curiously. "And how do you know this in such detail? Did Bertie tell you all about it? I assumed he was watching from some hidden place."

Fiona tugged playfully on Edward's scrotum. "Keep it up. Yes, he was spying on them. And Bertie kept a diary of such encounters, in code. I deciphered it one rainy day."

"You are a clever woman."

She shrugged. "I had nothing better to do."

"And you are modest as well. But, dear Fiona, would you lift your dress for me again? I feel odd being so naked and you not. And that way you can touch yourself if your story arouses you too."

"Very well," she laughed. She got onto her knees and pulled up her fresh dress, baring her arse and cunny without a trace of self-consciousness.

He stared at her intimately and she could see his cock twitch. "Hold it tightly," she instructed, "and pay attention."

Fiona leaned back on her elbows and lolled with her thighs open, giving him the full show he seemed to crave. "But don't touch—me, I mean."

He inclined his head in an affirmative nod, sliding his strong hand up and down his shaft and looking between her legs as he did so. "Go on," he said softly.

"Unable to stand there a moment longer and only watching, Danny came around in back of Shelagh and grabbed her tits, lifting them high and squeezing them hard. She struggled free and slapped him even harder."

"He deserved it," Edward said. "A perfectly ironed shirt is a beautiful thing. A masterpiece of domestic art, in fact. He should not have interrupted a dedicated laundress at her task, no matter how magnificent her tits were."

"Oh, shut up," Fiona laughed. "You will lose your erection."

"Nothing to fear. Your story is having its desired effect. There is the first drop, Fiona. Lick it up." He cupped the back of her head and gently brought her down to the head of his penis.

She darted out her tongue and took the salty–sweet drop, making an *mmm* sound and waiting for another. Just inside the head was a second drop and when it rose, she licked it too, sticking her tongue tip into the small hole and making him gasp. "Ahhh. That was almost painful. But I liked it. Now go on."

"Oh . . . where was I?"

"Danny had just taken a hard slap."

"Yes—and it hurt. But he seemed to enjoy it too. He dropped to his knees in front of Shelagh and humbly begged her pardon. She slapped his face again."

"And then?"

"He murmured that he deserved strict punishment and that he wanted her to do the honors. Shelagh just stared at him for the longest time, walking around him in her drawers a few times. Then she kicked him in the arse with her booted foot."

"And why did she wear boots if she was so hot?"

"To protect her feet from the puddles of scalding water, Edward. I take it you are not familiar with the hazards of laundry rooms."

"No, I am not."

Fiona contimued. "The coachman flinched and nearly fell but asked politely for another kick. She gave it to him."

"Did she ask why?"

"Indeed she did. She was quite curious. Then Danny began to whisper his story . . ." Fiona leaned back and spread her legs again. "Don't touch me," she reminded him. "Just look while I talk."

"Yes, my beauty," Edward whispered, stroking himself again.

"Danny stayed on his knees in front of Shelagh, looking up adoringly as if she were a goddess. And from his point of view, she was. Her legs were very long and her hips curved like the sides of a ship, flowing into a narrow waist that needed no corsets. Above that, her big, naked breasts rose proudly upon her chest. She stood with her hands on her hips, as Danny looked up.

"Shelagh gave him a look of pure fury mixed with puzzlement. 'Why would a big fella like ye want to be on his knees to me? I want to know . . . and ye're going to tell me. Or I'll have to smack the answer out of ye.'" Fiona looked at Edward, who was keeping a tight, almost protective grip on his hard member.

"He must have secretly enjoyed the discipline he received as a lad, especially if a woman administered it. Perhaps a governess took him in hand," Edward murmured, "Being forced to admit one's sins, bare one's arse, and endure sweet pain—well, some women are very good at giving that."

Fiona nodded. "That was essentially what he confessed to Shelagh. I am making a long story short."

"Please don't," Edward said.

"It is my story and I will tell it my way," Fiona said rudely. "Do not interrupt. Anyway, Shelagh picked up the paddle she used to stir the laundry and waved it under his nose. 'Is this what ye want? Shall I paddle yer arse fer ye?'

"Danny looked about the room and saw the double-sided drying rack, a sturdy contraption made of solid oak. 'If you would bend me over that,' he whispered, 'and tie my hands and feet to it, if that is your pleasure, I would be most obliged. Please punish me as you see fit.'

"Shelagh, filled with sudden power and rather enjoying herself, agreed to that. The coachman stripped and stood before her. Though he was taller than her and certainly much stronger, strong as she was, he wanted only to abase himself—to feel that she had overpowered him and not vice versa.

"His cock stuck straight up against his belly as Shelagh stared at him, a cold contempt in her green eyes. 'So it's punishment ye want, is it, Danny? Then punishment ye shall have.'

"She grabbed a length of clothesline, and wrapped it around his waist, then made a loop, which she cinched snugly around his bollocks. Then she drew the remaining length through his thighs and slid it through the crack of his bum, none too gently, tugging on it until he yelped, relishing the pleasure that such intimate pain brought him.

"Shelagh held him by this restraint and shoved him to the rack, ordering him to bend over it. He obeyed, thanking her for using her womanly strength to beat out his wickedness.

"She told him to shut up and kicked his feet so that they were wide apart and tied each ankle with a rag to the drying rack. Then she tied his wrists to the other side of the rack. She reached between his legs and gripped his dangling balls from behind. Danny moaned with pleasure.

"She tugged on the rope between his buttocks and tightened the loop around his balls. Danny moaned again. His cock stuck out between the rods of the drying rack, stiff enough to hang a towel on. Shelagh walked in front of him and showed him the paddle. 'This is what you want, is it?' "

Edward clasped his own stiff flesh and nodded at Fiona to continue. His face was flushed. She rather doubted that he would enjoy such treatment himself, but he did seem to be enjoying the story.

"Shelagh slapped the paddle against her hand, letting the coachman know that he was in for it. He begged for her to begin. Then the door to the laundry room opened and two kitchen girls came in. Young women, really, of nineteen or twenty, I do not remember."

"Inexperienced," Edward murmured.

"Well, no, as you will hear. They looked at Danny, who had never had a kind word for them, and then at Shelagh, who explained everything.

"The maids laughed as they looked at the coachman, naked and vulnerable, tied to a drying rack with his buttocks spread wide and his balls tightly roped, but his cock only grew larger. Then the trio of women whispered to each other and the two maids took off their clothes, quite quickly."

"Poor Danny," Edward said.

"Hardly. He was getting what he wanted—and what he deserved."

"I suppose you have a point, Fiona. Do you mind if I . . ." He slid two fingers into her wet cunny without waiting for an answer.

"Ahh . . ." She leaned back, surprised by the sudden thrust but enjoying it very much. "You were not supposed to touch me."

"But I have. Now go on." He slid his fingers in and out in the same irresistibly sensual rhythm as he had used before.

"The naked maids went head to tail, tongue-fucking each other's pussies right under Danny's nose, and making a lot of noise. But Danny heard Shelagh walk around and stand in back of him, leaving herself plenty of room to swing the long-handled laundry paddle. 'Please,' he whispered. 'Give it to me.' The tall laundress gave him his first stroke, a cracking good one that reddened his arse. Then a second. And a third. His buttocks trembled. 'Again,' he whispered.

"Shelagh paused when the maids got on all fours in front of him, showing him their bums and everything between, jostling each other like a pair of horses. Danny stared at their rumps, unable to touch, extremely aroused by the rude remarks they made to each other and to him.

"'D'ye want the privilege of kissing our arses, Danny?' one girl asked. He was past words and only nodded. The maid stood up, hands on her hips, and impudently brushed her bare buttocks against his face as Shelagh laughed at the sight.

"The more Danny was humiliated, the bigger his cock got. Shelagh gave him a few more strokes, then stopped, knowing he was close to climax. 'On yer knees, girls!' she commanded the maids. 'Show him what ye do in private in yer little room in the garrett—them beds are too small to turn around and what can ye do but play with one another?'

"The maids fell to their knees and locked themselves in a passionate embrace, pressing their firm young breasts together and rubbing slowly, lightly pinching each other's nipples and kissing wildly, lips apart and tongues in deep."

"Mmm," Edward said in a growl. "I like that picture very much indeed." He pulled on his throbbing cock. "Do you want to suck me?"

She shook her head. "My story is not finished. The kitchen girls were just getting started. As they kissed, they began to fondle each other's bums, pushing their hot cunnies together in just the way that a man fucks a woman. Danny was gasping and even Shelagh stopped to watch them at it.

"They turned slightly so Danny would get a full view of one

girl's behind as her amorous companion reached around to spread her soft cheeks open and then press them closed, again and again.

"'D'ye like that, ye little bitch?' Shelagh asked the maid who was receiving this attention. She clung to her friend and moaned a yes long and low. Vigorous and sustained squeezing of the buttocks can produce a climax all on its own, you know."

"Then I must do that to you, Fiona," he purred, keeping up his stimulation of himself and her.

"Later." Fiona patted the arm of the hand that he had inside her, liking the feel of his hard muscle and liking the sensual thrusting of his fingers even more. But she did not wish to come—no, that she wanted with Edward's huge cock rammed up inside her and him on top.

He touched her pleasure bud with the pad of his thumb and Fiona shook her head. She grasped his wrist and pulled his fingers out. Edward touched his cunny–slicked fingertips to her lips. "Taste yourself, my darling." She darted out her tongue to do so, then moved his hand to his own mouth, smiling. He licked his fingers as well, sighed with pleasure, and then settled back into the pillows.

"Shall I go on?"

"Yes." He cupped and rubbed his balls, for a change from the cock stroking.

"Shelagh squatted next to the girls to fondle the breasts of one and then the other, pinching a nipple when she could get one. 'I am next," Shelagh proclaimed, 'And I want my bum squeezed very hard. Like you just did to her.' She had forgotten all about paddling Danny. The maid whose attention the laundress desired waved her friend to one side and told Shelagh to kneel upright in front of her so that her buttocks would be soft, not tensed and spread as they were when she squatted.

"Shelagh did, still clad in drawers and boots, although she was so much taller than the maid that her bare breasts pressed into the girl's face. The maid paused to take in the sight, then clasped each tit, but Shelagh's large breasts were not easy to hold. The laundress gave her face a playful slap. 'Ye can do better than that. Now suck me tits. One by one.' The maid hung on and bent her head down to nurse upon one breast with strong sucks until the nipple was long and very pink. 'That's better,' Shelagh said, approvingly, arching back a little to enjoy the sensation.

"The eager maid let the nipple pop out and provided the same attention to the other, only stopping to draw breath and wipe off her wet mouth.

"'Now do me bum, if ye please,' said the imperious Shelagh. 'Squeeze it like I said.' She pulled the maid roughly against the front of her long body, smiling when the maid's face sank between her breasts. But the girl clasped her buttocks and began to squeeze and part them just as she had done before. The way the split in Shelagh's muslin drawers gaped to reveal her innermost parts was quite delicious. The maid pulled on the soft fabric, providing extra stimulation by using it for a good cunny rub.

"Danny could see that the fabric was soaked by her feminine juice. He made some comment to that and Shelagh turned her head, telling him that she would tie her dirty drawers around his face. He nodded eagerly, his eyes glazed by the constant barrage of erotic stimulation he was experiencing.

"The second girl watched her companion pleasuring Shelagh, admiring the laundress's magnificent bottom, which was quite muscular for a woman, though very round.

"'Spread her wider,' the girl said softly to the maid who clasped the laundress. 'Stretch her arsehole a little more with each parting of the buttocks and close it tightly with each squeeze. I found that very pleasurable—'

"'Did you?' her friend interrupted in a muffled voice, then pulled her head out of the cleft of the laundress's bosom, looking flushed, her face damp from Shelagh's hot sweat. 'Then come and kiss me—no, kiss me and her.' She caught Shelagh's indignant look at the distraction from her personal pleasure and the kitchen maid began again to work conscientiously on the laundress's behind. Then the female trio shared a three-way kiss, tongues meeting in midair and then plunging into each other's mouths at random, giggling from the sheer joy of being so naughty.

"Danny stared and stared at the wanton women, his cock already beginning to pulse without anyone touching it. Shelagh saw his excitement and rose to check his bonds, jerking on the loop around his balls and making him cry out.

"The two maids resumed the position they had been in before but traded places. The one who had been squeezing was now the squeezed. The girl was wildly aroused, especially when her obliging friend stopped and brought a finger to her mouth, knowing that all were watching her suck it. She pulled it out with a pop and then she stuck it in the other maid's mouth and let her suck it too.

"Staying with Danny, Shelagh watched the finger play, keeping a strong, capable hand on his paddled arse and stroking him absentmindedly. The coachman's powerful body trembled at her unexpected gentleness and he grimaced, fighting for self-control. 'May I come soon, Mistress Shelagh?' he asked.

"'Oho. *Mistress* Shelagh, is it? I do like the sound of that.' She patted his bum affectionately. "Ye and I shall have to do this again, Danny. But no—ye may not come. Control yerself or I'll give ye such a paddlin' ye won't be able to sit a horse for a week.'

"'If that is your wish, mistress," he replied, looking at what he could see of her—mostly her hips and cunny—from his tied position. 'A fine, sore arse will be my dearest remembrance of you—and a necessary reminder that I am at your service day and night. You may beat me at any time. I cannot say no.'

"Shelagh nodded. 'I must own that I like this game, Danny,' she said. 'Now watch the girls. I knew that they were lovers but not that they were such sluts.'

"The coachman picked up his head just as the maid reached around and stuck her slippery finger into the other's arsehole. Eyes wide, he watched her push it in slowly, past the first knuckle and then the second until her entire finger disappeared up her friend's soft arse. The penetrated girl cried out with pleasure and Danny bucked.

"Shelagh picked up the paddle and down it came again upon his quivering buttocks. His cock jerked, issuing spurts of hot come upon the naked girls, on the floor and down his leg. 'Spraying on the floor? Ye are no better than a dog!' she scolded him. 'And ye will be punished like one!' She whacked him once more and Danny groaned so loudly that the rafters rang. Shelagh made sure he received a stroke of the paddle for each violation of the cleanliness of her laundry room . . . and then told the girls to lick him nice and slow. He was in heaven."

Edward dropped his thick, twitching cock and arched his back against the pillows, clutching the sheets with both hands. "If I am not careful, I will come without permission as well."

"See that you don't," Fiona said with mock severity. But she did want to touch the huge shaft that stood up so proudly from his groin, showed to advantage by the way he sprawled with his thighs open. She dearly wanted to ride it. Just . . . not yet.

Edward sighed and she saw his taut belly relax a little. "And did Shelagh paddle her accomplices for a grand finale?"

"No. They ran off, gathering up their clothes—and bumped into Bertie, who came out from his hiding place. He rewarded them in golden guineas, much to their delight. Then he praised Danny for his stalwart submissiveness, promised him an extra week's pay as a bonus and told Shelagh to let him loose."

"What did she get?"

Fiona laughed. "A good fucking from Bertie, cheered on by

his coachman, who stood to watch as he could not sit, and a hundred pounds for her savage ingenuity. Bertie had a soft spot for hard women."

"Ah," said Edward. He stretched and rolled on his side, taking her hand and kissing it. "You have a rare talent for strange stories, Fiona. I must confess that that scenario excited me, although I have no wish to be tied to a rack. Still, Danny's delight in being dominated is not uncommon."

He fell silent for a moment. "La Belle Dame Sans Merci. A beauty without mercy. I have seen such a woman give the ultimate in pleasure to a willing man."

Fiona sat up, slightly piqued, not really wanting to hear anything of his past. Certainly he had many lovers, as had she—but she wanted him all to herself at the moment. She sighed and tried to sound nonchalant. "Shall I tell you another?"

7

"Please do, Mistress Fiona."

Fiona sat up and patted his cheek. "Oh, don't call me that. I have no wish to dominate you, Edward."

"Ah, well. I am up for all sorts of pleasure, as you can see." He indicated his erection, then clasped it firmly. "Hmm. Here is another drop for your tender tongue to savor. I shall be spurting as uncontrollably as the coachman in a minute."

"Then rest," she advised. "Your feelings of arousal will only deepen. You will come very strongly indeed when it is time." She bent forward to lick up the pearly drop, loving his soft murmur as she did so.

"Ah . . . since you speak of it, I have lost all track of time. I know that we sat down to dinner at eight and rose from the table at nine–thirty, but I seem to have been moving in a dream ever since. A very sensual dream."

"It is well after midnight, I think. I heard the bells ring once." She stroked his legs, wanting only for him to stay, even to sleep with her in a blissful post–coital knot of arms and legs and intermingled breath. "Must you go home?"

"No. No one awaits me, if that is what you are really asking."

She shook her head. Pride would not let her admit that. Yet certainly she had wanted to know during the last three weeks whether Edward had someone else. Of course, there could have been any number of reasons why he had kept his distance at first. He had wanted to wait, he was wary by nature, and so forth.

Fiona let her gaze move over his long body, well satisfied with the sight. He seemed disinclined to be anything but naked, anywhere but here. She reminded herself that it was never wise to ask too many questions of such a man. Wary? Perhaps the word for him was wild. The slightly wicked gleam in his eyes, the way he laughed, like Lucifer himself—but Lord Delamar was a very good-humored Lucifer, come to think of it.

And the way he made love—oh, oh, oh. She would never get enough, she feared.

"My dear, the hour is late. Are you too sleepy to tell me another story?"

Fiona came out of her reverie. "You are insatiable."

"Where you are concerned . . . perhaps. I have never had the pleasure of hearing such wicked tales from so charming a lady, you know. What is this one about?"

"Ah . . ." She tried to collect her wits and think of something. Not everything she had read in Bertie's journal was erotic. Fiona realized she might have to rely much more upon her imagination for this one. "It is quite different, I promise you."

"In what way?"

"Oh, it will be as sensual as the others. But no more servants."

"But I have enjoyed them all—the penitent coachman, the randy butler, the naughty maids, the lesbian laundress—quite a cast of characters, Fiona."

She shrugged. "I will return to them on another night."

"You are a veritable Scheherazade."

Fiona smiled. Should she tell him that was exactly who she had intended to be? She decided against it, especially since she was having the devil of a time coming up with her next story. However had the harem slave of legend come up with one thousand and one stories? Well, *her* life had depended on amusing the sultan, if Fiona remembered aright.

"Begin," said Edward. "Cast your spell. I am ready. But I cannot promise not to touch you this time. Your voice is entirely too suggestive and the tales you tell are too outrageous."

"Very well." She was pleased by his compliment but could not let it distract her. The thing to do was imagine the most beautiful and sensual women that could be imagined—*Scheherazade, help me*, she thought wildly. Then the answer came to her in a flash. The women of the harem, of course.

"Thank you," she said aloud, appreciating that little bit of magic.

"What?" Edward said.

"Oh—my mind was wandering."

"You are tired. Come and rest in my arms. And do take off that dress once you have locked the door. We are safe here, are we not? And quite alone. The household has retired for the night and I could steal away before the sun comes up. Or not, if you wish me to stay."

"Yes." Her heart leaped. So he wanted to be with her as long as possible—the feeling of sweet warmth at hearing that flooded her heart and surprised her by its strength. But she composed herself and saw to the door, and her undressing, pleased by the fire that burned brighter in his eyes when he saw her completely naked.

She got back in the bed and let him hold her, resting her back against his chest, encircled by his warm, lightly furred arms.

"Now begin. Or we shall both fall asleep and I don't want to. Not before making love to you once more. Possessing you fully. I have waited long enough and so have you."

"Yes, my love," she said softly.

He adjusted his position to look down into her face. "Am I your love? Oh, no—I should not have asked the very question you asked me."

"The reply will be the same. Do you want to be?"

His answer was immediate. "Yes. I do."

She turned around and kissed him long and tenderly. Then she looked into his eyes and he didn't look away but captured her gaze with his. For a moment, their souls were as naked as their bodies—a nearly unbearable moment for Fiona.

It was too soon for all that. She rolled around to face away from him but still let him hold her, relishing the feeling of his large, strong body curled around hers. *That*, above all, was irresistible.

"So. You promised another story, my lady. Am I to hear it while looking at your back?"

She turned in his arms, laughing. "It would be the same story."

"But I would not have the pleasure of watching your pretty lips while you tell it, and seeing how your eyes glow."

Fiona kissed his mouth but only fleetingly. "Bertie had a friend—an adventurer named Fitzroy."

"Bertie again." Edward sighed and settled her on his arm, tracing a line down her bare arm with a finger.

She launched into her tale without a second's delay. His tenderness might well undo her—and she had no wish to be undone. "Fitzroy traveled throughout the Ottoman Empire, offering his services as a translator to sultans and the like. He made himself useful, amassed a fortune over time, and was even permitted the rare privilege of visiting palaces where no other Europeans went."

"Not the harems."

"No. But Fitzroy eventually gained the confidence of one vizier, who brought him into the house of the eunuchs, who guarded the sultan's odalisques."

"Poor fellows."

"There was one among them who was not castrated, a young man who had been captured with a Moroccan beauty only a few years older. He was never allowed inside the harem proper, though she visited him from time to time, being apart herself from the odalisques and not one of the sultan's favorites."

"Then why was she there?"

Fiona smiled. "To teach the arts of love to the new girls, of course. Though most are rarely visited by their sultan, who has only a few favorites."

"Saving his strength, no doubt," Edward chuckled.

"Most of the odalisques had only fantasies of pleasure—and each other."

"I have heard as much," Edward said thoughtfully.

"Through the vizier and the Moroccan woman, whose languages he knew, Fitzroy learned so much about the harems that he wrote a book—a scandalous book privately circulated here. The illustrations revealed that hidden world in every detail: the beauty of the pampered and bejeweled odalisques and their personal slaves, the strict hierarchy in which they were ranked, the exquisite costumes that displayed their shaved cunnies and perfect breasts for all to see—all who lived within the harem walls, that is—and, of course, their sexual practices."

Edward grinned wolfishly. "My, my. I must read it. Is there a copy on the shelves of your library, Fiona? Or do you keep it under lock and key?"

"No. And I am not sure where it is." She waved a hand airily. "I will look for it if you like."

He laughed. "Not now. But if you would promise to read

from it as we examine the pretty pictures, I shall look forward to that."

"I promise." Fiona smiled and continued her story. "Fitzroy was the agent of an earl who wanted a harem woman in the flesh."

"To bed or to wed?" Edward inquired.

"Both, as it turned. A white one and a dark one—harem women were from many lands. He desired his own, just as some rich men must have giraffes or other exotic creatures to show off as curiosities and proof of their wealth. Fitzroy introduced him to a minor sultan, a practical fellow who sought to reduce the size of his harem by selling a few."

"Barbaric," Edward said firmly.

"Hm. Considering that the usual method of disposal was to tie the unwanted ones into sacks and drown them in the Bosphorus, this sultan was considered quite humane."

"Fie," Edward said. "But go on."

"Andrews bought two women, the Moroccan one and the blond odalisque she attended, who was some years younger, perhaps twenty or twenty-one. The sultan threw the young man into the bargain."

"The one who was not a eunuch."

Fiona nodded. "The earl was entranced with his new toys. The Moroccan woman had dark doe eyes and tawny skin, and the bearing of a queen—a most beautiful and exotic queen. The other had very white skin and fair hair. They had been inseparable since the day the blond girl entered the harem. No one knew where she came from."

"Why not?"

"She was quite deaf. She and the Moroccan communicated by signs of their own devising that no one else understood."

Edward settled her more closely into his arms. "And were they lovers?"

"Women in the harem sometimes became very close, or so

Fitzroy explained to Bertie. Some were lovers, certainly—and like most men, the sultans loved to watch amorous women kissing and fondling each other's breasts and playing with each other's cunnies.

"The harems were rife with jealousy and violence. But many of the women looked after each other, cherishing their friends so intensely it seemed that they were lovers. Their constant intimacy meant that nothing was secret. Harem women bathed together for hours, attended by female slaves of lesser rank, who scrubbed and oiled their beautiful bodies once a day, and dressed their hair."

"Hm," said Edward. "You have not quite answered my question about the women the earl bought, Fiona. But I expect you will. Oh, and do give this trio names, or I will never be able to keep the story straight."

"Nakshedil was the name of the Moroccan. And the blond girl was called Sevim."

"And the young man?"

"Hamed. The earl brought them to England and installed them in his house in the country."

"A sensible decision. He would have been asked far too many questions in London. I wonder what his servants thought of such exotic creatures."

Fiona thought of her own servants and their pretended lack of interest in her affairs. In the months since her husband's death, she had amused herself with Thomas and two other lovers of whom Thomas was unaware—and since his departure from her life, Lord Delamar.

Certainly Sukey must know something of them all. Was it foolish to think that the maid would not? It seemed to Fiona that the girl had become noticeably bolder of late, and perhaps she had gossiped—but what did it matter? Fiona was not received everywhere, but she scarcely cared.

She forced her mind to return to the story she was inventing to titillate her new lover, improvising from what she remembered of Fitzroy's book and her own treasured volumes of Oriental fantasy tales, privately printed with women in mind, which she had not shared with Bertie.

"As far as Nakshedil was concerned, Sevim belonged to the earl and so did she, according to the customs of the harem."

"And Hamed?"

"He served Nakshedil faithfully and obeyed her every command. Fitzroy, who had returned to England with Lord Andrews, said he could count himself lucky."

"The earl quizzed Fitzroy endlessly on harem customs, and asked him to translate what the women were saying. Bertie, who knew Andrews well, was also eager to learn their every little secret. But, despite Ftizroy's urging, Nakshedil was not inclined to converse and knew no English in any case. Sevim was unable to talk at all, of course.

"Nakshedil was very protective of Sevim and kept her close by her side. The girl had been sold as a virgin, for a very dear price."

"Is that so very different from England?" Edward mused. "When did you lose yours, Fiona?" He slid a hand down her belly and let it rest in her damp curls.

"That is another story," she laughed, "and I am not likely to tell it to you or anyone. I lost it too soon, if you must know. But that was long ago."

"Yet there is something innocent about you still," Edward said softly. "Yes, you like to play the wanton but even so . . ." He didn't finish the sentence but held her close.

Fiona twisted in his arms to look up at him, puzzled. "What the devil are you talking about?"

"I think it is love that you have never experienced."

"Perhaps. But I have experienced everything else," she said dryly.

"You are cynical," he sighed. "Cynical but beautiful. Do go on with your story."

"The women were never apart—in fact, they almost clung to each other. Bertie, the old sneak, paid a maidservant on Andrews's staff handsomely to spy on them and report every detail to him when Fitzroy proved less than helpful."

"Filthy-minded old bastard," Edward said.

"Hypocrite. You are enjoying the details yourself."

"So I am." Edward gave Fiona's cunny a friendly squeeze.

"The earl's exotic new pets loved nude bathing and all that went with it. They spent hours taking care of each other's bodies, as harem women do. And Hamed had been trained as a masseur, a skill he now practiced upon the Moroccan woman, since there was no one to tell him no."

"You mean cut off his balls."

"Well, yes. But he never touched Sevim, reserving that pleasure for his Moroccan mistress. Then one day . . ."

"Torture me. Go ahead." Fiona felt Edward's cock growing in size against her back and rubbed herself against it.

"Nakshedil, in the nude, was massaging Sevim, who lay on her belly, rubbing her down with fragrant oils until her bare white skin gleamed. When Sevim sighed with contentment, kicking her pretty feet in the air, Nakshedil treated her to a foot rub, oiling and pulling on each toe as Sevim wriggled with pleasure. Then Nakshedil took her by the ankles and turned the younger woman onto her back.

"Sevim opened her legs at once, as if she had been trained to do so. The spying maidservant was shocked to report that Nakshedil looked closely at Sevim's cunny, playing freely with it and spreading the lips. What she didn't know was that the young man was not far away, hidden from the women behind a curtain."

"Then who did know he was there?" Edward murmured.

"Forgive my interruptions, but the people in this story seem to appear and disappear as if by magic, Fiona."

Help me again, Scheherazade, she thought. Fiona was having a little difficulty keeping track of this one herself, especially since she was making it up at breakneck speed. "The earl could see all four of them from his partitioned hiding place. He wrote it all down and shared it with Bertie later. He'd had the bathing chamber specially built for the women and wanted to see for himself what went on there, having heard Fitzroy's tales of naked odalisques disporting themselves in the steaming water while the sultan watched. And being scrubbed and oiled and shaved and plucked.

"You know, of course, their religion says hair upon the body is sinful and they remove it all by various means. Sevim's nether lips flushed a deep pink under Nak's probing fingers."

"A delectable contrast to her white skin," Edward said lasciviously. "I would like to lick her myself.

"Oh, do shut up. Sevim seemed not to mind Nakshedil's looking at her private parts—no doubt it had been routinely done in the harem. She clasped her legs behind her knees to lift up her buttocks and show everything."

"And what did the young man think of that wondrous sight?"

"I was just getting to that part, Edward. The earl wrote that his cock and Hamed's stiffened simultaneously. He watched the young man take out his member from his loose trousers and stroke it slowly from base to tip, over and over.

"He stroked faster when Nakshedil stretched the blonde's nether lips gently, spreading them to reveal Sevim's hymen, the precious proof of maidenhood. She even touched the delicate membrane with a fingertip to ensure that it was intact.

"The young man swallowed a moan and let his flowing come spurt freely upon the floor some distance in front of him, giving his ejaculating cock hard, frantic strokes. Hamed was still entirely unaware that anyone was watching him but he continued to stare intently at Nak and the young woman she attended until he squeezed the last drops of hot fluid into his hand, breathing fast.

"Sevim trembled. Nakshedil withdrew her finger and folded the outer lips shut. Then the blond girl reached out her arms to the dark woman and caressed her with ardent affection."

"So they were lovers."

Fiona shook her head. "Sevim trusted Nakshedil, who in turn trusted Hamed—and no one else. They only had each other. And they needed each other. Sevim had spent most of her young life in bondage and now had been taken to a distant country from which she might never escape. Nakshedil, older and wiser and accepting of her fate, was duty-bound to prepare the virginal Sevim for what would pass for a marriage.

"But, as Fitzroy found out later, Hamed, who had grown to young manhood under his countrywoman's protection, was madly in love with Nak, because of her kindness to him and to others.

"It was well-known in and out of the harem that Nakshedil had kept others from preying upon Sevim, or hurting her. The girl's deafness made her a target for cruel teasing."

"No doubt Nak had saved Hamed from a far worse fate."

"Yes. When Sevim's pale beauty aroused the jealousy of others, the sultan thought it best to sell the lot of them."

Edward nodded thoughtfully. "I suppose Nakshedil thought of the earl as the sultan and Fitzroy as a vizier."

Fiona patted his brawny chest, feeling the heart within it beating in a slow, powerful rhythm. "That is why she confided in him, in Arabic, which he understood well. He then wrote down their story, and so did the earl, and Bertie had a version of it from the maidservant—oh, dear. It is getting very complicated."

"But quite enjoyable, Fiona," Edward said. "Stroke me, my love, while you talk," he said softly.

She trailed her fingertips over the swollen, silky flesh. "Nakshedil indicated that she wanted Sevim to massage her, and the naked girl jumped down from the table and let her beloved friend climb on and lie down. She poured oil into her cupped palm, trickling it over Nakshedil's back and rubbing it in. Then she reached lower and slowed down, taking her time to extend her strokes down the other woman's thighs, covering every inch of bare skin with the warmed oil."

"Every inch," he sighed.

"Her white hands moved over Nakshedil's tawny body, treating her rounded, beautiful buttocks with particular tenderness, smoothing oil upon them and rubbing it in."

Fiona began to stroke Edward's cock in earnest. It was so hard it had to ache. But he only smiled sensually. "Tighter. Hold it tighter." She clasped him firmly.

"When Sevim had finished, the other woman rose from the table, her tawny skin shining, looking at Sevim's body with desire. Nakeshedil's beautiful doe eyes were filled with love—and passion. She took the bottle of oil and dripped more upon her breasts, rubbing in circles as Sevim watched. It was obvious that she was teaching the blond girl how to arouse herself—and how to arouse a lover.

"Sevim stared at her friend, mesmerized by the sensual show. Then Nakshedil offered her breasts to her, cupping them from underneath, and spoke softly, letting Sevim read her full lips. The blond girl understood at once—and so did Hamed, who was instantly erect once more, his stiff rod rising over his bare balls and his trousers fallen halfway down his thighs."

"I can imagine it," Edward interrupted. "Tighter, sweet Fiona. Hold me ever tighter. I want to come upon your belly while you talk to me and stroke me."

Fiona reached her curled fingers under his bollocks and stroked him there while she pulled on his huge, hardened cock. "Sevim put her hands over Nakshedil's erect nipples with a look of wonder as Nak pushed her breasts out, letting Sevim rub her heated flesh. The gentle fondling gave the Moroccan woman very great pleasure, and excited the innocent Sevim beyond measure.

"The blonde put her mouth upon one long nipple and then the other, suckling as Nakshedil stroked her fair hair. They felt no shyness and no shame. Hamed, watching from the shadows of the curtain with no one to help him ease his heated flesh, was ready to explode.

"Oh, yes." Edward groaned, shoving his hips—and his throbbing member—at Fiona. "If only we had oil. I would like to see you rub your breasts until they gleamed. Tease me mercilessly and be a perfect bitch about it. Push your hot nipples into my mouth and let me suck while you ride me from above."

Fiona let go of him and turned to the nightstand. "Perhaps there is some in here. Bertie made sure to stock the rooms with whatever guests might need." She scrabbled through an odd assortment of stuff and came up with a small bottle of liquid, which she uncapped and sniffed. "You are in luck. It is oil and it is still fresh."

"Then use it on me. Use spit. Use anything. I want to feel what those women felt. Soft hands upon my most sensitive skin."

Fiona poured a few drops, just enough, into her palm and carefully applied it to his penis. She stroked him from the base to the tip, pulling down the foreskin on her first stroke and exposing the head. She squeezed the shaft in a pulsing rhythm and slid her hand up and down it.

"Ahhh . . . ohhhh . . . .please stop! I will come too quickly," he moaned. "Just tell the story."

She let go, wanting to finish the tale quickly so they could get to real fucking—hard, cunny-pounding pleasure—at last.

"Sevim dragged the huge Turkish towel from the table and put it on the floor. Then the women oiled each other all over again, from belly to bum, and gripped each other like wrestlers."

"Greased, naked, beautiful wrestlers," Edward said. "My God, you are good at this game, Fiona."

She winked at him, pleased by the compliment. "They fell upon the floor, straining sensually against each other, sliding off and grappling again, laughing in a wanton way.

"The display of writhing female flesh—and velvety pink, shaved cunnies revealed when thighs opened to clasp thighs—was something to see. Hamed wrapped his arms around his chest, not touching his member as he watched, wanting to make the pleasure of seeing women's naked bodies locked in amorous battle last as long as possible.

"Then Sevim scrambled on top of Nak when the other woman was on all fours and clasped her around the waist, gripping Nak's arse with her legs and riding her playfully. Young and slight as she was, Sevim was no match for the Moroccan woman's superior strength.

"Nakshedil reached back and grabbed Sevim's ankles, bucking her off and flipping her down upon the Turkish towel. Sevim was panting wildly but eager for more of such exciting roughness. Nak forced her soft thighs apart, fondled her hairless cunny, then flipped her over and slapped her snow-white arse as well, leaving pink marks upon it and kissing each one. Sevim pushed her bum up shamelessly, asking silently for even more of this pleasurable punishment. Nak immediately gave the young woman what she wanted but could not ask for."

"Was such play enjoyed in the harem?" Edward said. "And I thought only the English relished it."

Fiona paused in her stroking, thinking up an answer. "Nakshedil saw nothing wrong with using her hands upon the bare flesh of misbehaving women who were sent to her, because she knew that most enjoyed it. And she never left a mark upon them. As I said, the sultan who owned her and Sevim permitted his odalisques a few liberties."

"Bizarre. But intriguing, I must own."

"Where was I? Oh, yes. Nak versus Sevim. The wrestling match continued. The Moroccan woman pinned the struggling blonde and forced her thigh between Sevim's white ones. The girl grabbed Nakshedil's flexed buttocks, making her wince, so deeply did Sevim's nails dig in."

"Ahh," said Edward moaned. "Describe every detail. I love a good cat fight."

Fiona continued blithely on, pleased with the success of her outré tale. "Still clutching Nak's behind, Sevim raised her legs as she had done to have her private parts intimately inspected—the moment that had triggered lustful feelings in both women—and threw them over Nakshedil's back, crossing her ankles tightly to force the other woman's cunny down upon hers. Suddenly one juicy pair of nether lips pressed against the other and the fighting women rubbed their hot pussies together."

"And Hamed?"

"He still would not touch himself. He watched Nak thrust her hips down between the younger woman's and begin to undulate slowly, her rounded buttocks shifting and rolling.

"Sevim responded fiercely but had no words to express her sexual longing. Dark and light, the women moved as one, consumed by the intensity of their secret desire. Nakshedil began to slide her body over her Sevim's, pressing up and down over the point of utmost pleasure in her lover's virgin cunny.

"Hamed stood stock still as Sevim pulled Nak's head down for a rough kiss, wanting those full, tender lips to violate hers. The women kissed passionately as Nakshedil's downward thrusts upon her lover's shaved, sensitive cunny became more vigorous. Sevim clung to her as Nak cried out her excitement.

"Nakshedil writhed in orgasm and Sevim's eyes widened. She caressed her lover's back and arse, and let Nak raise her shoulders so she could tease her dark nipples and fondle her breasts. Then Sevim felt the thrill of her first climax seize her body and shake her from head to toe.

"Spent, the women fell apart, bestowing tender kisses all over each other's bodies. Then Nakshedil remembered her duty, and got up to crouch between Sevim's legs and gently spread her lover's throbbing nether lips to look within. Once more she touched the delicate hymeneal membrane with a fingertip. Sevim trembled as before, knowing that this bit of flesh would be saved for the man who had bought her. But Nakshedil comforted her by signs and soft words, and then sent her off to bed . . ."

Edward sighed, his eyes closed and his straining cock twitching in her hand. "What a story. I hate to hear it end."

"It is not over. Have you forgotten Hamed?"

"No."

"The young man came out from behind the curtain and begged Nak to give him the same pleasure. She stretched out on the towel, letting him look at her dripping cunny while he pulled off his trousers and shirt. He kneeled humbly between her legs, then bent forward to penetrate her fully with his tongue, lapping up the juices of the two women's lovemaking like a worshipper at a secret shrine.

"She clutched her hands in his black hair, keeping his face in her cunny, enjoying her power over him, and crossed her ankles in the air. When his whole body was trembling and his cock leaking the first drops of come, Nak pushed him up. He grabbed his cock and plunged it into her, screwing in deep while she played with his buttocks. She reached around to put an oiled finger into his tight arse while he writhed. The young man, accustomed to such treatment from time to time in the darker corners of the sultan's vast palace, wanted his dear mistress to give him erotic penetration as well, of course."

Edward groaned. "Then what happened?"

"They came together and then vanished in a puff of smoke, and went back into the genie's lamp, my lord."

He opened his eyes. "Do you mean to say that you were making it all up?"

Fiona's voice was soft. "There was some truth in it. Fitzroy's book is real, and he told beautiful stories of love between harem women and the few men that they knew. I added a few embellishments, to be sure."

"Enough." Edward rolled her over and used his muscular legs to get hers apart, bracing himself atop her. The tip of his cock bobbed against her cunny lips but he waited, savoring the anticipation of that first thrust. She ran her hands over his broad shoulders, down his arms and up again, delighting in the sight of his powerful body over hers. "You have told me everything I need to know about you."

"Whatever do you mean?" He was quite wrong. Fiona had no intention of letting him get the upper hand this early in the game—or ever.

He laughed a little and turned his head to kiss her caressing hand. "You are a pretty thing but an argumentative one, to be sure."

"I am not."

He lowered himself upon her but not all the way, keeping his cock back and making her squirm with frustration.

"I know that you like to watch the intercourse of others—very much—even though you pretend that you never have. And that the sweetest delights seem to come in threes in your stories," he purred in her ear. "And, my darling, you like extremes . . . of tenderness and violence. The idea of being pleasured by a female lover intrigues you but I am not sure that you like such company otherwise. You are very much a man's woman, Fiona."

She made no response, embarrassed that he was able to read

her so easily, but she said nothing. She was aching to thrust up against him, to take his cock deeply within her, but she knew he could easily dodge her.

"And you have had many men. Three since your husband, if the gossip is to be believed—"

Piqued, she slapped his face and immediately regretted it. Edward grabbed her wrist and held it against the bed, keeping his full weight off her by supporting himself with his other arm. "So it is true."

"What of it?" She should not feel such annoyance that people talked about her, and even shunned her, but she did. After all, he was no better. Fiona was not about to change her ways to suit convention.

"Fiona, I would not presume to judge you because you enjoy the same freedom I do. You must promise one thing, however."

"I do not make promises," she said with venomous softness.

"Listen to me before you say no, Fiona. You are a man's woman—but I want to be the only man in your life. Say yes." His dark eyes burned into hers with fierce intensity.

"Give me one good reason to say yes," she whispered, trapped by the strong hand that still clasped her wrist. She feared it would break if she wrenched free, so tightly did he hold her.

Edward rammed his cock in hard, all the way. "There is your reason, my lady." The fire in his eyes was worthy of Lucifer indeed. He rested within her for only a few seconds, than began to shove himself in and out, filling her cunny completely with each thrust. Teasing her nether lips with the silky, dripping head as he pulled back.

Aroused far more than she had realized by the telling of her sensual inventions—and his passionate response to them—she suddenly felt a powerful orgasm pulse through her. Fiona screamed with pleasure too deep and strong to comprehend. The room around her seemed to dissolve . . . to the point where there were no walls . . . and then no boundaries between her and her lover. Only his body, claiming hers. Only his lips. Only him.

8

Edward lowered his head to hers, kissing her with infinite gentleness, his momentary flash of anger over. No doubt he thought he had conquered her, Fiona thought, not ready to believe it. Her body still shook from the force of her orgasm. Yet she felt ashamed to have come so readily for him, unwilling to admit that her desire for him had been so strong.

He rocked between her thighs, sliding his huge cock in and out, enjoying her swollen sex and the last pulses of her climax. "Ah, Fiona," he whispered against the side of her face. "Making love to you is so sweet. And you are so hot inside. I can feel your excitement—I know you want more."

She shook her head, almost on the verge of crying. Never had she wanted a man so much, nor had she understood that a man might have the power to make her want him. To allow that to happen was to make herself extremely vulnerable.

But her body had not lied. The powerful climax that had shaken her to the core meant only one thing. *This man and no other*. Now that she'd bedded him she could never be satisfied by anyone else. Damnation!

No one would have a chance, of course. Edward had no intention of permitting her to pick and choose among the handsomest men in London. She was to be his, and his alone. He would have it no other way.

Yet she could never control a man of such magnetic sexuality. He would never be entirely *hers*. As strongly as she now desired him, as shaken as she had been by the intense orgasm she experienced when he entered her at last, she knew that falling in love with him was a dangerous proposition.

It was not something she could think about while in his embrace, her body enfolding his. He had the advantage of uncommon sexual skill—a weakness of hers where men were concerned. She had the disadvantage of being perilously close to an emotional surrender she had not expected. Fiona closed her eyes and a weary tear ran down her cheek. He felt its warm trace and raised his head, brushing the tear away.

"What is the matter, love?"

"Nothing."

"You came so quickly. And that was your second time."

He resumed his thrusts, giving her strong pleasure she was reluctant to feel—yet it thrilled her. The thickness and length of his cock and the way he wielded it might have any woman on her knees begging for more.

Fiona put a tentative hand upon Edward's back and then another, feeling the play of muscles as he moved above her and in her. Excited despite herself, she savored the feel of his large balls upon her arse cheeks with each deep thrust in. Edward had an iron cock—and iron self-control.

Self-control that she evidently lacked.

Yet he did not have to know that he had stirred her emotions so violently—without even trying, damn him. To protect herself from now on, she would have to hide her feelings carefully. The fact that she had given herself away for even a second and shed a telltale tear troubled her.

Fiona concentrated fiercely on something else, casting her mind back to the masturbating woman she and Thomas had seen in the house across the street enjoying the slap and sway of her heavy bollocks and the deep penetration by her dominant lover. Edward was right. Fiona did love to watch. And she did love extremes. And the idea of bringing other women into the mix did intrigue her, but only the idea.

Nonetheless, if she were to fantasize one while Edward fucked her, it might be an effective shield against his unexpected power over her—and his disarming tenderness.

So . . . she concentrated even harder, conjuring up a threesome. Her lucky number . . . for fantasies, anyway. The woman she chose to share him with—and vice versa—would love to see everything that Edward had swinging between his legs coming down hard between Fiona's while she waited her turn. Edward was not likely to be shy about doubling up, if it came to cunnies that needed fucking.

Fiona put her hands on Edward's buttocks and held tight, spreading him a little and thinking about a second woman kneeling on the bed between his legs and playing with his balls.

The thought aroused her. She would not share it. Then she imagined getting on all fours next to another woman, also on all fours, while Edward spread the woman's cunny and rammed into her hard and slow, then changed to swifter strokes while he kept one hand on Fiona's behind, telling her she was next. Watching a lovely woman rock back and forth beside her, tits bouncing from the vigorous fucking Edward was so good at would be delicious.

Before he came, Edward would pull out of the other woman, slick with her juice, and fuck Fiona, saving the best for her. He would ask that the women kiss while his cock was deep inside her and thrust away, until their new partner decided to lie underneath Fiona and apply her tongue to Fiona's dripping cunny and his dangling balls. She would take a breath only to beg

Fiona to suck her juicy pussy too so all three of them could climax simultaneously. Edward would be unable to control himself and . . .

The raunchy fantasy was working. Fiona dug her nails into his buttocks.

"I like it when you hold onto my arse and drive me into you, Fiona," he whispered. "Let me hold yours." He slipped his hands under her bottom and tipped her hips up, driving his engorged flesh ever deeper.

She wanted every inch. His strong fingers almost encompassed her arse cheeks, which he began to squeeze.

"I know you like that," he gasped out. "Ohh . . . but I don't want to come . . . not yet!" He squeezed her arse faster and harder, driving into her, and Fiona almost climaxed for a third time. She pushed him away, whispering, "Turn me over. Take me on all fours."

He gasped and rose from her, letting her get quickly upon her knees and wasting no time in thrusting inside. Fiona could feel him extremely well in this position. She put her head down and reached between her legs to touch him and herself, using her own slipperiness to lubricate her fingertips. She felt his scrotum tighten suddenly and his balls rise around the base of his huge cock as it slid in and out.

Then there it was . . . that incredibly intense feeling that only he had ever given her . . . she screamed with pleasure and thrust back, back, back. "Oh, God, yes! Harder! Yes!" She cried out again and felt him shudder as a powerful climax coursed through his body and hers.

He gripped her hips and his flowing semen filled her cunny and splashed onto the bed below. "Sweet woman . . . what you do to me . . . oh . . . ohhh!" He gave a final thrust, then pulled out and collapsed next to her, still fully erect. "I'm done for." He rested a hand upon his chest and drew her down to his side with the other, encircling her from shoulder to waist.

Almost unwillingly, Fiona nestled against him, listening to the strong beat of his heart, deeply soothed by it. And suddenly loving him more than ever. Damn, damn, damn.

Loving him was a secret she would have to keep. She was far too vulnerable—and quite unable to keep him at a distance. And should she ever have to tell him her other secrets, he would not want to be her love much longer—something she could not bear.

She stilled her restless thoughts and sank into a troubled sleep by his side.

9

Wandering with him down a series of corridors and finally turning left, Fiona brought Edward into a windowed hall that overlooked the stables. The staircase at its end led outside and was an ideal place for him to make an inconspicuous departure.

It was nearly dawn but Fiona checked to make certain that no one was about. The low building and its wide doors were clearly visible in the moonlight that sparkled on the wet cobblestones of the drive.

Had it rained? Apparently so. A fast–moving summer shower had drenched the city and freshened the night air, and then let the moon rule the sky, now lightening in the east, for a little while longer.

Edward surveyed the stable with interest. "Quite large for London."

"Bertie kept three carriages and the horses to pull them, as well as mounts for himself and me."

"His lady wife," Edward said. His smile was ironic, made more so by the faint scar near it.

"I never thought of myself that way."

"Why not, Fiona?" He seemed inclined to tarry now that their mutual passion had been taken care of. She didn't mind.

"I was born a lady but a poor one, and as far as being married to Bertie—it was not my wish, but my father's."

"He was a gambler, or so I have heard."

Fiona raised an elegantly arched eyebrow. The never-ending gossip—why did he have to bring it up? She almost wished Lord Delamar was able to satisfy his infernal curiosity in some other way. Alas, she had few secrets and her father had a reputation as a rotter.

"Not *was*. He is. And he always will be. Papa cannot seem to stay away from the tables," she replied at last. "He is utterly improvident but still quite charming in his way, though I daresay my mother would not agree after living with him for forty-odd years."

"And where is your mother, Fiona?"

"She lies abed all day, daydreaming and playing solitaire when not quarreling with the servants," Fiona answered curtly. "Mama and Papa have only a few servants left. They stay on because they are too old to go elsewhere."

"How sad for them all."

"Must we talk of such dreary things?" she said.

"No. Forgive me." He drew her to him and planted a lover's kiss on her forehead. "You look tired."

"I am . . . but no woman ever wants to hear a man say that."

"You look beautiful and tired."

She laughed softly. "That's better. To hell with the truth."

He bent down to nuzzle her neck. "Fiona, you are a delight. When may I see you again?"

"Whenever you like." She descended with him down the rear staircase and opened the door that led to the street. He gave her one more tender kiss and then he was gone.

Two weeks later . . .

Fiona and all her servants had removed to the country to escape the summer heat of London. They were residing in a dreary pile of stone, Bertie's notion of a charming rustic retreat, which also served as the summer residence of an infinite number of spiders. Everywhere Fiona walked, she seemed to encounter a spongy web across her face, despite Mrs. Geffrye's valiant efforts to clear them away with a broom.

The housekeeper shouldered this weapon each day, followed by Henchley, who carried an old shoe for squashing purposes. Sukey refused to help them—she rarely left the small chamber that had been assigned to her at all. The lady's maid was sulking, no doubt over having to leave her mystery lover behind in London, where she thought he might be up to his usual tricks—but with other women.

Fiona had given up on scolding her, because she too was pining for a man: Edward. She had penned several amorous missives to him since their arrival, but had not walked to the village to post them, and did not trust the servants to do it for her.

She brushed an ambling spider from the folds of her dress, well past shrieking about such things. In the event of a letter from Edward announcing a visit, she would change her clothes, but not otherwise. She had worn the same damned dress all week, since anything she sat down upon was quickly smirched with dust and mold.

Summer holidays were a grim business. The thought of knocking this ghastly pile down and rebuilding from the ground up was tempting—perhaps a pretty cottage with glass-paned doors flung open to catch the hay-scented breezes of the English countryside. Perhaps not. The cows might wander through the drawing room and she could not imagine Mrs. Geffrye going after them with a broom.

Without friends or family about, Fiona was lonesome. Even Harriet had gone elsewhere, and was now somewhere in Devon, painting watercolors and eyeing the brawny yeomen in the fields while Ned napped the afternoons away.

But Fiona was determined to make the best of it. There was a library upstairs that did not seem to have quite as many proliferating spider webs as the rest of the house. She might have a look through the books and see if there were any novels to read.

Fiona went out the front door and looked about. A patch of straggling primroses was all there was in the way of a garden. Certainly that was a pastime that many people enjoyed, but not Fiona.

How she looked forward to autumn and her return to the city. Sukey's brooding and door–slamming when she thought her mistress was out of earshot was irritating the other servants, who thought she was shirking her duties. The girl seldom spoke to anyone but Mrs. Geffrye, and was rude to her at that. But the housekeeper was tired of her impertinence and Henchley, who was moody as well, was growling about putting Sukey over his knee and giving her "what for."

Fiona heard the distant clatter of carriage wheels and turned her head to look. She was not expecting visitors, Edward had not written, and she thought the equipage would drive on. But the carriage turned right, racketing down the overgrown drive that led to the front of the house.

She peered into the leafy shadows. It was a hired carriage, by the looks of it, driven by a London hack with an unkempt beard. He pulled up the horses and brought the carriage to a halt. Fiona nearly screamed when Edward swung open the door and stepped out. She ran into his arms. The hack fiddled with the reins and occupied himself as best he could, discreetly ignoring their warm reunion until Fiona let her lover go.

Edward gave him double the fare. The hack's eyes widened

and he touched an imaginary hat in a gesture of thanks before helping another man, evidently Edward's valet, down from the other side. The valet collected the bags and went on ahead.

"You did not write, Edward," she said breathlessly. "But I am so glad to see you." She brushed back a trailing lock of hair. Sukey had done it up quite carelessly, although Fiona had not minded that until this moment. But Edward seemed delighted to see her all the same.

"I came out straightaway, darling. I thought you would rather see me than have a letter from me, so here I am."

She twined her arms around his neck and kissed him again, even more passionately, standing on her toes.

"Are you alone?"

"In a manner of speaking. I am surrounded by bad-tempered servants, but I wish I weren't."

He looked curiously at the stone pile. "So this is the house. It is . . . picturesque."

"It is dreary!" she burst out. "I hate summer, I hate spiders, and I cannot wait to leave! But now that you are here, at least I have company."

Edward turned to see that the hack driver was well down the road. "I told him not to wait."

Fiona threaded her arm into his. "Fie. We shall amuse ourselves somehow, my darling." All her doubts about loving him had vanished during their separation, as if the summer heat had melted her fears. Her cherished independence had one very great drawback: there was not an endless supply of men like Edward, and all others paled by comparison. She had missed him. She did want him.

"I expect we will." His tone was lightly teasing. "Have you more wicked stories to tell me?"

She shook her head. "There is a library upstairs. We might find something worth reading, I suppose."

Fiona opened the creaking front door and led him into the

hall. This was hung with gigantic antlers, and bits of armor, and mildewed paintings of robust barons whose names she did not know.

"Charming," Edward said with a gallant smile. He waved to his valet, who was still stacking the bags. "Where is the footman?"

"Summers ran off with a tavern wench but there is still Henchley. Ah, here he comes."

The tall butler entered the hall almost noiselessly, and bowed to Lord Delamar. Henchley frowned at the sudden clatter coming from the hall and the sound of women's voices, high and quarrelsome.

Edward's valet looked up. Light female footsteps heralded the arrival of Sukey, who ran into the hall but stopped short when she saw the valet.

"Jack!"

"Hallo, Su." The valet looked at her nervously. "Well, fancy meeting you here. Himself said we was going to the country but not where. I am surprised."

Sukey crossed her arms over her chest, looking as if she wanted to ask him what he had been doing and who he thought he was, but Henchley's glare made her hold her tongue.

"They seem to know each other," said Edward with dry amusement, taking Fiona several steps away and speaking so softly only she could hear him.

"We're in for it if they do," Fiona whispered. "I knew she had a new man, but not that he was your valet, Edward."

Sukey and Jack exchanged a look that boded trouble. Fiona and Edward exchanged a look of their own and left the servants to themselves.

Fiona allowed Henchley to lead Edward to a room once Mrs. Geffrye, flailing her invaluable broom, had readied it for a human inhabitant. Sukey had made the bed in slipshod fashion, Fiona noted when she went to visit him. Edward was already half–naked, scratching the fine dark hair on his chest and looking about.

He opened his arms the second he saw her, and she went into them, nestling against his heart.

"I had imagined you in a romantic bower, my love. Awaiting me with . . . open legs."

She laughed and gave him a hug. "Do you think of nothing else?"

"Do you, Fiona?"

"No."

"Shall we?"

"Yes."

He picked her up and kissed her lasciviously, then settled her bottom on the bed. "The day is warm. We will sweat like horses if we make love in the usual way."

Fiona wriggled and pulled up her dress from under her bum. He looked at her with a wicked grin. "No drawers, I see."

"No." She fell back on the bed and let her knees fall open. "Put your mouth on me, Edward. Lick my cunny."

Breeches on, chest bare, he knelt before and applied his tongue to her at once.

Some hours later, they sat down to dinner, an odd assortment of dishes that Mrs. Geffrye had prepared earlier, before she ran out of stove wood. Henchley had been sent, grumbling, to scour the spinneys and copses for more, and had only just returned, his arms laden with long branches. The window was open and they could hear the dull thuds of an ax and his curses.

"Oh, dear," Fiona remarked. "He sounds like a murderer. Would you like some salad, Edward? Or plain bread and butter? The aspic has melted and the meat pie is impenetrable."

He poked a tarnished fork into the pie and pried up a large piece of thick crust. "Mrs. Geffrye did her best." He took a bite of the cold filling. "Entirely edible. I will have the pie."

Fiona settled for salad and bread fetched from the village a day ago, chewing it vigorously. "What news from London?"

"Not much, my dear. Everyone who is anyone is away at some fashionable retreat or gone to the country, like you. Oh—before I forget, I did want to ask you about something."

She paused before taking another bite of bread. "What?"

"You said Bertie kept a journal. What happened to it?"

"I don't know. It is among his papers, I suppose. His solicitors have all that. The last time I saw the journal was a few months before he died. It was on his desk." She popped a morsel of bread in her mouth and chewed thoughtfully. "Why do you ask?"

"It has been mentioned in connection with a blackmail case. No doubt some important people would like to know if their extramarital affairs were recorded in it. He spied on your guests as well as your servants."

"I don't remember telling you that."

Edward shrugged and took another bite of the thick-crusted pie. "Such secrets are difficult to keep. Bertie was garrulous to a fault, and he told other people of the journal."

Fiona put her fork down. "Since I deciphered the code, I do know that he left me out of it. As for the rest . . . some of it was true and some of it was invented. One never knew which was which with Bertie. He was a liar."

"And not a well-liked man."

She shook her head. "No, he was not. I have no fond memories of him. And the idea of ever having another husband seems quite impossible, thanks to him."

"You have me," Edward said.

"Indeed I do. And you are not the marrying kind. Nor am I." She smiled at him, glad to have said it straight out.

"Hmm. Well, as you are independently wealthy, also thanks to Bertie, you need not worry on that score, my lady."

They finished the meal in a companionable silence.

Several hours later . . .

Though every window was open, the house was stifling. Edward turned over restlessly, damp with sweat. Fiona, who had stolen into his bedroom and was lying beside him, blew a soft breath over his back.

"Ah. If only there was a breeze. I cannot sleep."

She wanted to curl around him, but she was as sticky as he was. The day's heat had settled in the upper story of the house and had not dissipated in the cool of the night. The moon's blue light poured into the room and Fiona could see him frown.

"Nor can I, my darling. But the moon is full and we might wander outside if you like."

He sat up, running a hand through his tousled hair. "Very well. I shall lay you down upon sweet grass and—no, it will be damp."

She rose and slipped her light dress over her head, tugging it down. "Straw, then."

He found his breeches on the floor by his feet and stood up to put them on. "Do you mean the stable?"

"That is where one usually finds straw, is it not?"

"As you wish. Straw is no bed for a lady, though." He donned a loose linen shirt.

She gave him a mischievous smile. "I shall be on top, Edward."

Barefoot and laughing softly, they arrived at the stable some minutes later. Edward swung open the half-door, which creaked loudly enough to wake the dead. The stalls were dark and there was only a soft whuffle here and there from a dreaming horse to let them know they were not quite alone.

But the grooms slept in a nearby outbuilding, Fiona knew. They were safe enough.

He swung the door shut and fiddled with the latch. She put a foot on the first rung of the ladder to the hayloft, and went up. By the third rung, Edward was at the bottom of the ladder and caught her by the waist, settling her on his shoulder. He held the ladder with one hand and steadied her with the other as she clutched his hair, giggling. The old stable was low-walled and the ladder was short.

Fiona scrambled off once she was through the opening to the hayloft and stood up carefully, not wanting to crack her head on the heavy rafters. But a whooshing sound startled her and she flinched as a large owl, just as startled, flew out the window on wide wings.

Edward was just in time to see it go. "I should have gone up first and looked about. I am sorry, Fiona. Are you all right?"

"Yes, of course. It surprised me, that was all."

He took her into his arms and kissed her gently, brushing her tumbled hair back from her face. "An amorous woman by moonlight. Is there a more beautiful sight on earth?"

She kissed him back.

"Where shall we lie, my love?"

Fiona clasped his hand and looked about. "In the loose straw."

He let go, squatting to heap up the straw and then dragging a bale over next to it. "There. A backrest."

"You think of everything, Edward."

"But I did not bring a sheet."

She reached down, picked up the hem of her dress and pulled it over her head in one swift motion. "You can lie on my dress and roll your shirt into a pillow for your head."

He clasped her waist, admiring her nakedness in the pale moonlight for a moment before he bent his head down to kiss her again. He took off his shirt and tossed it onto the straw, then undid his breeches and hung them on a nail.

Fiona pressed her body to his, standing on her toes to rub her nipples against his chest hair. The tickle was delightful. He murmured something wicked and grabbed her arse, picking her up off her feet and burying his face in her breasts. She cupped one and gave him the nipple to suck, watching it disappear between his lips and sighing at the tender sensation.

"Mmm. Nice numples," he said indistinctly. He let the sucked nipple go and moved his mouth to the other one. Fiona touched the wet flesh and tugged at it while he put his mouth on the unsucked nipple, murmuring silly things and making her wriggle with laughter in his strong arms.

Still clasping her by her buttocks, he let her slide down his length. Fiona paused to drop a kiss upon the head of his cock, already touched with a drop of creamy come for her, and spread out her dress upon the straw for him to lie upon. She balled his shirt and put it at the top.

"My lord." She indicated the improvised bed. He stretched out upon it but she stayed standing, wanting to admire the gorgeous male body she was about to ride upon.

"Look your fill, my lady. You know it arouses me when you stare at my cock. I can't help it." Edward's shaft bobbed as it rose up, stiffened by desire. He clasped it and stroked himself with luxurious slowness, looking up at her with heavy–lidded eyes.

Fiona slid her hands down to into the nest of curls between her legs and found her pleasure bud. She stroked herself with her forefinger, curling the others into her palm, only stopping to tug it gently between her thumb and forefinger, when the stroking became too intense. She wanted to make this last, especially since he had already pleasured her—royally—with his soft mouth shortly after his arrival. But he had not come. His balls must be close to bursting with hot juice by now.

"Ah, I love to see you play and pull upon on that little thing," he murmured. "Stand with your legs farther apart, if you please. The moonlight silhouettes you very nicely."

She did as he asked.

"Do women ever think about having what men have?" he inquired softly. "A rod like this?" He slid his hand up and down. "It would make their naughty play with each other much more interesting."

"Of course we do. Women employ all sorts of such toys. Ones that can be held in the hand and rammed in, and ones that strap on. And women who love women enjoy giving penetration as much as they do licking cunnies. You are a man of the world. You know that."

"But I want to hear you say it. Tell me more."

Fiona paused in midstroke with her fingertip just touching the head of her clitoris. "Let me sit down by you. You can rest your head upon my thigh and watch me pleasure myself better that way."

She knelt near his head, then folded one leg and settled down, leaving the other knee up so he could see well. He waited for her to get comfortable, then put his head down only inches away from her cunny. Fiona put her finger back where it was. She began to stroke the hot little bud that he gazed upon and watched him pulling on his hard, huge cock. He was handling himself more roughly now, excited by her willingness to talk of women's secrets.

"I am sure you have heard of Lady Raynald, my love. A habitué of stables and a connoisseur of horseflesh . . . and pretty women."

"Yes." His voice was ragged.

"She loves to dress as a young man and tuck a strap-on into her breeches to make a fine show. A friend of mine—a married woman but a lover of her own sex, like her husband—told me that Lady Raynald had one that hung halfway down her thighs."

"That is too long for pleasure," Edward murmured.

"And too thick. She wears it for effect. To inspire a proper attitude of submission, I think, in her female lovers. Lady Raynald likes to tell them what she will do to them with it, just as if she were a man." Fiona's cunny-stroking finger moved faster through her curls, slicking her bud.

"Go on." He stuck out his tongue and gave Fiona a quick, exploratory lick. "You are very hot. Inside and out."

"Yes. But I have to stop touching myself—I want to come with your cock inside me, Edward." She withdrew her hand and stroked his tousled hair.

"Will you imagine that it is Lady Raynald's dildo inside you and not me?"

She murmured soothingly. "Of course not. You are all I want."

"But if the fantasy excites you, then think all you want of her and Sapphic sport while I fuck you, Fiona." He gripped his cock hard, squeezing the sensitivity out of it by applying pressure under the head with his thumb. "Ow! I have to make it hurt a little, darling. I am too close to coming."

He let go of his penis, which remained just as stiff as before.

Fiona continued. "Lady Raynald once cropped her hair very close, playing the part of a young groom, well-hung and randy, to satisfy the whim of a demanding little beauty of her acquaintance. They met in a stable, of course. Lady R wore a man's shirt and buckskin breeches, which she let down to show her strap-on, telling her lover in a rough voice to take it into her mouth and wet it thoroughly. The young woman pulled up her riding habit to show her lacy, feminine underthings and knelt to touch her tongue to the leather rod."

"Oh, no . . . I mean yes. Go on." Edward turned his face against Fiona's thigh and muffled a moan. "This is your best story yet. Let me rest . . . please. Talk of something else. No, don't. Just explain why men are fascinated by tales of lesbian love."

Fiona patted his cheek. "Because women are much wickeder

than men seem to think—and they know just how to stimulate the imagination. Yours is at fever heat right now."

He reached down and gave his cock another hard squeeze under the head. "There. I must not release too soon. Now go on."

She smiled. "Lady Raynald's strap-on had a large bulb at the top and a shaft as big around as a man's finger and thumb in a circle. It did not look much like a cock once it was outside her breeches, but the sensation it provided was even better.

"Lady Raynald demanded that her lover suck harder. The young woman was barely able to open her pretty lips wide enough, but she licked it with devotion while Lady Raynald thrust the thing into her mouth."

Edward groaned.

"She looked up and smiled when she was done, and turned around, crouching on a bale of straw. Lady Raynald grabbed her by the hips, pushed her riding costume higher and ripped her lace drawers open. She spread her pretty companion's arse cheeks, touching the bulb to her private parts. Little by little, enjoying the view from behind, Lady Raynald let her lover's cunny open up around the thing. The roundness and its unusual size were extremely stimulating, judging by her little cries of pleasure. But the shaft was still outside her cunny.

"'Give it all to me, milady,' her lover moaned. 'It is so satisfying to be fucked by a woman in breeches . . . your rod is much bigger than any man's . . . but I want you to possess me completely. Push in hard. Please, my darling. Please, oh please.'

Lady Raynald held the little beauty's hips even more tightly and positioned herself while the woman moaned and wriggled her cunny lips around the bulbous tip. She thrust in of a sudden, filling her lover completely, cupping the young woman's buttocks with capable strength that was indeed nearly the equal of a man's.

"She spread her lover's soft arse wide open, and looked

down to watch the leather dildo go in and out. The young woman rocked back and forth, clutching the bale of hay, shameless and wild for more pleasure.

"Lady Raynald's strong hand slid over a hip and down into her lover's glistening curls. She pinched and pulled at her clitoris, crying out, 'Ah, you are a beautiful bitch—and a hot one!' "

Edward rolled away and stretched out, his cock huge, its veins pulsing, straight up against his taut belly. "No more. Ride me, Fiona." He reached out to her and half-dragged, half-lifted her on top of him. She grabbed his cock and put the head between her cunny lips, positioning herself for a downward thrust that would get every bit of his gigantic erection inside her.

One second later, she shoved her arse down and he bucked wildly, holding on to her hips so tightly it almost hurt, shooting hot jets of creamy come against her womb. She rocked and rocked, rubbing upon his aching balls as he moaned. Fiona came just as hard, crying out his name.

10

And back to London . . .

The weather had changed. The oppressive heat of summer was pushed aside by several days of drizzling rain, during which Fiona discovered that stone leaked.

Or rather that the slate tiles of the stone house in the country leaked. She decided to leave the place to the spiders and told Sukey to pack up. Mrs. Geffrye bustled about getting everything else into boxes and bags for the carriages and the large wagon her mistress had ordered sent from London to bring them all back to civilization. And not a moment too soon, in Fiona's opinion.

Edward had stayed for two days but had to leave to see to matters of pressing importance, or so he said. She missed him very much. The servants were no substitute, and their constant quarreling—even though they fell strangely silent the second she entered a room—was wearisome.

Thrilled at first by the unexpected arrival of her mystery lover, Sukey had spent a day and a night in bed with the man and then barricaded herself in the well house after a screaming fight. She refused to come out until Edward and his valet left. Henchley muttered darkly about throwing her down the well to save himself the time and trouble of doing her in by more elaborate means, but nothing came of it.

The maid was simply impossible, and Fiona planned to sack her upon their return to London.

As for Henchley . . . well, the imperturbable butler seemed perturbed indeed. Away from his customary routine, he plunged into beetle–browed gloom and Fiona found herself edging away from him when they chanced to meet. He had taken to talking under his breath . . . about her? She could not make out the words.

She would have liked to ask Edward for his advice on the matter, but Edward was miles away.

It was time to return.

The first of the carriages stopped in front of the Mayfair mansion, and the new footman, hired from the village inn, jumped out. He took Fiona's hand and assisted her to the curb. She was glad to be home; and even more glad that she'd had a carriage all to herself.

Sukey had been forced to sit silently between the stalwart shoulders of Henchley and Mrs. Geffrye in the second carriage. The butler had threatened her with a demotion to the wagon, open to the elements although their belongings were covered with canvas, if she did not behave.

Sukey flounced up the stairs, snagging a few of Fiona's lighter bags, the jewellery case, and a hatbox. Fiona followed, letting Mrs. Geffrye oversee the unloading, wanting only to lie down and have tea and a light meal sent up to her room.

The elderly couple who had watched the house during their removal to the country could manage that, but Fiona did not want to ask the old women to climb all so many stairs. She would send Sukey down for it.

The house smelled odd when she entered, un–lived in and unloved. Not that there was much to love about it. The place reminded her far too much of Bertie and the décor reflected his pretensions. But the housekeeper would soon put it to rights, fling open the windows on every floor to get rid of the stuffiness and supervise the maids who had the miserable job of cleaning it.

Fiona mounted the stairs, looking from side to side upon each floor. The warren of corridors and rooms seemed overwhelming. It occurred to her that she ought to sell the place, pack up all the ancestral knickknacks, and move somewhere more pleasant. An elegant villa, just big enough for two lovers. She thought wistfully of Edward, knowing what a scandal it would be if they simply lived together and wondering if he wanted to.

They would not have to reside in London, of course. She was a wealthy woman and selling this monstrous house would make her wealthier still. They could always run away to Italy, bring the paintings by Tiepolo and Titian back to their native land, and live in a palazzo of golden stone.

She had seen one near Florence, a glorious relic of the Renaissance, while on the Grand Tour with Bertie. But the roof had long since fallen in and there were donkeys living on the first floor.

Still . . . Fiona sighed as her foot reached the topmost step of the staircase. Then she heard masculine footsteps coming up the stairs behind her and quickly turned with her hand upon the banister, hoping—absurdly—that Edward had come.

It was only Henchley, intent upon some household errand. Perhaps he was opening the windows in the attic to draw a breeze through the stuffy house. He nodded respectfully, not wanting to go ahead of her.

Fiona waved him on and turned toward her bedroom, hoping that Sukey had turned down the bed and opened the windows by now. The door stood ajar and someone was moving inside . . . a fleeting female shadow.

Fiona entered without Sukey hearing her and caught the maid with her hand in the jewellery drawer, a theft–proof, locked one built into a cabinet that Fiona knew she had locked as well.

"What? Where did you get the key to—are you stealing from me?"

"No!" With a pearl necklace dripping over her hand, Sukey's reply was hardly convincing. She crammed it back into the drawer. "I—I was putting this away. I brought the case upstairs with me. And you told me where the key was."

"I did not." Fiona was just too tired to think about it. "Or at least I don't remember telling you." She might have done, having no great regard for jewels and possessing far too many of them.

"You did, my lady," Sukey said stubbornly. "Or was it Master Bertie who told me where it was? Now I don't remember."

Master Bertie? Her late husband's oldest servants had called him that but the familiar appellation seemed odd coming from Sukey's lips. Especially since the old man had got the maid with child before she was eighteen and treated her with careless disregard thereafter. Fiona rather doubted that the young woman had been fond of him. "I am positive I did not—but we will talk of this later. Leave the drawer the way it is."

For a wonder, Sukey obeyed.

"Ask Mrs. McGillicuddy to prepare a tea tray and a little food, and wait in the kitchen to bring it up. She is too old to climb all those stairs. I fear that *I* am too old." She flung herself upon the bed.

"Not at all. You have Lord Delamar and he is devoted to you." Sukey's voice was oddly honeyed.

"Don't be romantic, Sukey, it doesn't suit you." The women exchanged cold smiles and Sukey left the room without a curtsey and without another word. Fiona unlatched the traveling jewellery case, dumped the trinkets in it into the open drawer, then shut and locked it and the cabinet as well.

She would have to take inventory. Then sack Sukey. Tomorrow. First thing.

Fiona got up an hour or so later, refreshed by the tea and sandwich Mrs. McGillicuddy had provided, and went out upon a minor errand, simply to smell the smell of London—which was unpleasant, certainly, but it was *home*—and soothe her soul with the clamor of its streets.

She returned before sunset and went to her desk, where she penned a brief note to Edward and rang for Sukey to give it to the footman to deliver.

The maid remembered to dip a curtsey this time, on her best behavior, which was more unnerving than her insolence. Fiona waited until the door closed behind her, then locked it. She sat down at her desk again and removed a small key, the one that unlocked the cabinet, from a hidden cubbyhole.

If Sukey had indeed known where it had been hidden before, that explained everything—except why nothing had been taken from the drawer. But Fiona's inventory had been entirely mental and she did not quite trust it, since she kept no written record of the pretty things that her lovers had sometimes given her.

So the maid's story might be perfectly true—or it might not. The guilty look in Sukey's eyes had to signify something. Fiona reached under the desk, feeling for a small panel that slid open at a touch and withdrew another key, the one that unlocked the jewellery drawer. She would go through the stuff once more and count every last pearl and bauble.

"Harriet, I do not know what to think."

Fiona sat on the edge of her bed, facing her cousin, who cuddled Beastie, ensconced in the large armchair she preferred.

"The girl is not listening, is she?" Harriet inquired, looking around as if Sukey might be hiding in a closet for all they knew.

"No. I sent her out upon my errands with the housekeeper, who will keep a strict eye on her."

Harriet nodded. "So you have gone through your precious things and nothing seems to be missing. Yet you found her hand in the drawer. Odd that Bertie would have told a servant the whereabouts of those keys. He at least knew the value of what he gave you, though you have never cared much for jewellery.

Fiona threw up her hands. "He liked her at first—and I assumed that he was the culprit when her pregnancy began to show. But he never seemed to pay much attention to her after that, and or to care when she gave up the child."

"What was it, Fiona? A boy or a girl?"

"A girl. Probably destined to follow the same path as her mother."

All women are destined to follow that path, unless we avoid pregnancy or sleep only with our own kind," Harriet pointed out. She gave Fiona a very sly look indeed.

Fiona sighed. "Now what? Have you and Ned brought a lass to your bed?"

"No, my dear cousin." Harriet beamed. "A strong young man."

"Then you had better be careful. Ned is virile, though somewhat past his prime. A young fellow produces bucketfuls of seed."

"Well, it's all in where he puts it, isn't it?" Harriet sat back and let Beastie jump down and walk about the room. The plump spaniel sniffed around the fireplace and lifted a leg, leaving a few drops of urine on the blackened bricks.

"Tell him no, Harriet," Fiona said indignantly.

"It is a very long way down the stairs and up again," Harriet replied. "And it is not as if we could send for Sukey to walk him."

Beastie sat down heavily on his rear and panted at them.

"Oh, look, he's upset because we are quarreling," Harriet said. "Poor Beastie. Poor plumpums. He is a sweet plumpums, he is. Sweet baby plumpums." The dog favored his doting mistress with an idiotic grin. "Aunty Fiona doesn't mean it, Beastie. Not a word."

Fiona shot them both an exasperated look and stretched out on the bed. "Never mind. I suppose it is expecting too much to ask you to discipline him, Harriet. You are not very good at that—"

"Oh! But I can be very strict. I was telling you about my young man."

"So you were," Fiona said dryly.

"He loves to be spanked by a mature woman—isn't that amusing? And he asked Ned to watch."

"Oh. Have you two no shame whatsoever? How old is the fellow?"

"Twenty-five. Tall and well-favored, with a boyish grin that just melted my heart."

Fiona's lips curved in a slight smile. "Certainly old enough to know his own mind. Go on, Harriet. And tell me where you met him."

"At Lord Camperdown's last assemblée. It turned into a minor riot, but it was great fun. He came up and introduced himself, and we were soon talking about very intimate things. The punch was very strong, Fiona."

"I see." Fiona settled her head on one outstretched arm, but kept an eye on Beastie, knowing that Harriet wouldn't.

"He confided in me that he preferred older women, because they understood that men sometimes had, ah, unusual needs. I asked him what those needs were, and when he explained—he was quite shy and very charming about it—I said I would be happy to do the honors."

"Then what?"

"He took me home, and Ned was there. He listened sympathetically and we all went upstairs, having hit it off. So to speak."

"Ha ha."

Harriet wriggled in her chair, remembering the evening with evident pleasure. "Of course Ned knew just what to do. The young men on his ships are often disciplined very harshly."

"The word is whipped."

"Well, yes," Harriet said blandly. "But our new friend only wanted a spanking. Ned told him to take down his breeches at once so we could see his manly parts. You should have seen the young man's cock, Fiona. So silky and so stiff! He wanted me to touch it and I did . . . then I gave it a spank. It became even stiffer and he blushed."

"I can imagine."

Harriet pressed her ample thighs together. "I sat down upon the side of our bed and told him to lie down over my knees and he did. His bare bum was lovely—muscular but just fleshy enough for good sport. I stroked the cheeks and made up some story about why he should be spanked."

"And what was Ned doing?"

Harriet looked thoughtful, as if she could not quite remember. "He looked on, that was all."

Fiona flopped on her back, imagining the scene and the happily married couple indulging in a tryst with a new partner. The Mellons were nothing if not open-minded.

"I could feel his swollen member right through my dress as he began to rub against my thighs. 'None of that, lad,' I said sternly. 'You must put your hot cock between my thighs for a proper spanking. Allow me to pull up my dress, if you please.'"

"So you were naked, too."

"Well, only from the waist down. He rolled off and I removed my drawers and got ready. Then I put him over my lap again and trapped his cock between my thighs, and patted his bottom gently. I had never done anything like this before, you know."

"It might be the only thing you haven't done, Harriet," Fiona said thoughtfully.

"Oh no, not at all."

"Get on with it," Fiona said, managing to look interested.

"By this time, my dear Ned had his own cock firmly in hand."

"Of course."

"Our handsome playfellow began to move vigorously up and down, begging with his bottom for a good session as he thrust between my thighs. My hand came down and I smacked him hard several times. He moaned about how soft my thighs were and how good it felt to be clasped so tightly and lovingly. I reddened his cheeks for him nicely as Ned cheered us both on. The young man bucked in my lap, 'That's the way, lad, Ned said softly. 'Enjoy yourself.'

"He moaned again, thrilled to indulge in his secret vice and be shared by a couple. Then the young fellow's eyes widened suddenly and he cried out, releasing his seed between my thighs when I spanked him very sharply. Ned shot his come right into my mouth. A neat job all around."

"And what about you, my dear cousin?"

Harriet waved a hand and smiled happily. "I took care of myself."

"You are good at that," Fiona said affectionately.

"Thank you, Fiona. I suppose I have to be, with a ship's captain for a husband. Anyway, I wriggled my bare arse upon the bed to make myself come while I was spanking Kingsley.

"So he has a name."

Harriet nodded. "Oh, yes. He is quite real, and that was a true story."

Fiona laughed. "I am sure that it is. And thank you for distracting me from my cares with it."

11

After midnight, in a remote part of the house . . .

Sukey, not wearing much besides an abbreviated corset and a short skirt that would have been indecent on a music hall dancer, pulled her breasts out and propped them up on the corset's stiff top ruffle. Her pink nipples showed to advantage, even by candlelight, and Henchley looked at them hungrily.

"So you were jealous of Jack, were you?" Sukey said softly. "Couldn't be helped. I knew he was Lord Delamar's valet but no one told me he was going to pay a call in the country. I suppose you think he came up wanting to bang my behind like everyone else."

Henchley said nothing but his face contorted in an ugly frown.

"Don't be cross. We're going to have our fun and play Master and Maid, just like I did with Bertie. Glad he's dead, I can tell you that."

She put a small, booted foot upon the first step of a ladder that the housemaids used to dust near the ceiling. "Liked to tickle my bare arse while I pretended to clean, he did. And my tits." She took another step up and reached for a feather duster that lay atop a bookcase. "He used this." She threw it at him. Henchley made a grab but missed, drawing in his breath as he watched Sukey mount the ladder.

She hoisted her skirt with one hand and held onto the ladder with the other, displaying her naked buttocks for the butler, whose face grew red. "What are you waiting for, Mr. Henchley? Go ahead. Brush my arse with the duster. Do a good job."

The tall man rose awkwardly, clutching the duster. She tucked the skirt between her knees and held onto the ladder with both hands, swaying her soft, bare behind back and forth, then bending at the knees and straightening up to stick it out. "Go on. You know you want to."

He brushed her buttocks while she giggled and shrieked. "It really does tickle, you know. Don't stop." She wrapped a leg around the side of the ladder to reveal the rearmost part of her cunny to his staring eyes. "Can you see everything, Mr. Henchley?"

"Yes," he growled.

"I know you like looking at women's private parts," she whispered. "You used to look at me through the peephole Master Bertie had put in the wall of the servant girls' room. I knew you were there. I was always thinking about your big cock in me when I was playing with myself. I wanted you to fuck me. And I want you to look hard at my cunny now that you can get as close as you like."

Henchley came closer and spread her nether lips roughly, putting his face near.

She felt his soft, hot breath on the inside of her thigh and pushed back an inch or two so that he could see even more. "That's right. You like the smell of a woman, Mr. Henchley. A hard–working woman like me. I'm not one of these dainty bitches who won't let a man put his nose near her golden cunny. I'm good and dirty. Clean me."

He gave her thighs and bare arse more feathery strokes while she murmured encouragement, then let his arm drop to one side, his hand clutching the duster handle convulsively.

Sukey turned around to see why he had stopped. "Shall I tell you what Master Bertie did with the duster?" She took it from him, putting the smooth round tip of the handle into her mouth and getting it wet. "He had me thuck it," she said around the handle. Then she pulled it out of her mouth. "He stuck it in my arsehole while I was on all fours and made me crawl around with it in my bum. It was very embarrassing but he paid me so much money I didn't mind.

"Bertie brought in a friend to watch with him once, and they both looked on while I got on all fours, naked as you please, to show them the duster rammed up inside my tight little hole. Bertie's friend wiggled the duster and made me diddle my cunny, then both men ejaculated on my back and behind. They spread their hot jiz around on my arse cheeks like jam on bread."

Henchley was breathing hard and beet red.

"Did you like that story, sir?" She gave him the feather duster, looking at him with an innocent pout.

She turned around on the ladder, pulling up her skirts in front and tucking the hem under the bottom of the corset to hold it. "Do my tits, big man. Tickle the nipples." She lifted her breasts out of the stiff corset ruffle and caressed them, pinching the nipples into hard pink points.

Henchley gritted his teeth and stopped to adjust the angle of the erection that swelled in his dark blue trousers.

"Look at that big thing," Sukey said. "D'you want to slide it between my tits while I kneel? Give me a good tit fucking. I would squeeze them around your cock extra-tight, Mr.

Henchley." She pushed her breasts together to demonstrate, creating a deep vee of flesh. "They look like an arse this way! A tight arse for you to spread." She pulled her breasts apart again. "Where's the little hole, eh? The one you grease and stick things in. Make a woman show you what she can hold in her arse to please you. Then stick your big hot meat in it and fuck the snug hole. But that costs extra."

"Shut up." Henchley stuck to his appointed task, applying the feather duster again to her bare flesh, running it over her shoulders and her neck as well as her breasts until she giggled even more loudly.

"Did you like that, Mr. Henchley? Do you want to feel my tits and suck on them? Please do. I am at your service, sir."

Her whorish talk was arousing him to the limits of his self-control. He dropped the duster, put his hands on her breasts, then nipped and suckled them like a starving man.

"Tits and arse, tits and arse," Sukey sang softly. "All the men want tits and arse."

He raised his head, gasping for breath. Sukey turned her back to him, flipping up the skirt again. "And now for the arse again. Touch me. Go ahead." She began to caress her own bum to encourage him, rolling her fleshy buttocks in an enticing way.

Henchley grabbed her so hard that Sukey stopped in mid-roll. "Now, now. No bruises on these peaches, if you please. But have a good feel."

The butler put his hands where hers had been and squeezed more gently.

"Do you know," Sukey said conversationally, "the disadvantage to beginning with a bare bum is that you don't get to take my drawers off. Should I put on a nice frilly pair and let you pull them down?"

"No," Henchley whispered.

"Oh, it's good sport. The drawers slide down and the arse

pops out. Sometimes they get stuck in my juicy cunny halfway down and then I have to be spanked for wetting them. Put me right over your knee, sir—I bawl like a baby when I'm spanked just right. And then you can put those big hands over my bare flesh and feel how hot my poor little behind gets from such treatment. Very hot, indeed, Mr. Henchley."

"No!"

"Thought you might like to, was all," she said huffily.

"Why waste time?" he said in a half-strangled whisper. "I have seen your arse and your tits. But not the inside of your cunny."

"Not yet." Sukey looked at his crotch. "Don't be shy, Mr. Henchley. Pull out your big thing and show it off. All the ladies love a big thing and I've seen yours before, but you were in a hurry, weren't you? Blast, you are shy sometimes. Let me." She clambered down from the ladder and briskly undid his trousers. His male member bulged inside his drawers, the last remaining barrier. Sukey's deft hands made short work of the buttons.

She pulled out his cock, which didn't bend. "Aha. Long and thick and hot. That's what I want. Every woman needs to be rammed by a cock like that. Put your money down and it can go into me right now."

Henchley shook his head and stepped out of his trousers and shoes. "Our game is not finished." He pulled off his shirt, for some reason no longer afraid to make a move and ready to play.

"What game?"

"Master and Maid. I want to do everything Bertie did. Everything."

"You are a wicked one. Very well. We've done the dusting—oh, I think we can skip the floor scrub this time. Very hard on the knees, that is, though Bertie loved to watch me get dirty when I did it naked. I suppose he told you."

Henchley made no answer and Sukey prattled on. "But he loved to bathe me afterwards and soap my cunny and arse very carefully. Then he rinsed me with fresh cold water until I was so clean I squeaked. And then . . ."

"And then?" The butler's voice was shaky.

She wanted to laugh at him, but not until after she was paid. "We'll talk about that when I've had my bath. Come along." Sukey took him by his big hand and picked up the candelabra. "Come. There is water in here. It's cold but we will manage."

Henchley followed her into the next room, looking at a half-filled tub, a big one, on the floor. There was a smaller one with low sides next to it that was dry but held a bar of soap.

Sukey set down the candelabra and shed her skirt. She strutted in front of him in just the corset and stubby-heeled boots. Her breasts overflowed the top and her bum swelled out below it. She put her fingers in her nether curls. "Nice and fluffy, they are."

"Yes," he whispered.

"Do you want to see all that when it's dripping wet? Let me get out of this corset." She untangled the knotted mess of laces and opened it but her breasts stayed high. "Ah. That's better. Now I can breathe." She flung the corset aside, turned her back to him and bent way over to unfasten her boot buttons, taking her time about it and giving him yet another show.

Henchley stared at her bottom and the cunny squeezed between its round cheeks, drawn to its irresistible juiciness. He dropped to his knees behind her and kissed her silken pink flesh, holding her hands to her ankles so she stayed bent over.

"Oh! Lick my cunny! Do, sir!" Sukey cried.

Henchley's tongue darted out and he tasted temptation. She wriggled and sighed in his grip, pushing her bum into his face as he kept her ankles and hands together. She let her head hang down and looked at his cock through the gap in her legs.

Assessing his state of arousal was easy enough. Sukey knew

he would not take long to come. The big, heavily veined rod twitched every time Henchley's tongue touched her cunny as if offering a salute of its own.

"Oo! Oo! Oo!" Her screams of pleasure had a well–practiced ring but Henchley didn't care. He let go of her ankles all of a sudden, then reached to catch her before she toppled over.

Sukey straightened, rubbing her lower back with a grimace. "That was harder than floor scrubbing," she muttered.

"What?" asked Henchley, dazed with desire.

"I said that you are harder than any man I ever knew." She pulled him to his feet. "Time to watch me play in the water, Mr. Henchley."

Sukey kicked off her unbuttoned boots and wiggled her toes. She walked past him to the tub and sat down in it. The water rose as her weight displaced it, and her breasts floated free, the nipples instantly erect from its coldness. He took a chair and sat beside her, soaking the cloth that had been hung over its side and rubbing it over every part of her body he could reach.

Sukey twisted and turned in the big tub, actually enjoying this part of her night's work. He was almost . . . gentle. She dreaded the clients she visited outside the Gilberte house. Some tried to scrub her flesh until it was sore and raw, and had to be hit with a shoe to get them to stop. Freelance whoring without a madame or pimp was not for the faint–hearted.

Doing Henchley now and then had been an easy way to earn extra money, since they lived in the same house. That he now seemed to think he owned her—well, that was just ridiculous. Tonight he wanted more, of course, and as long as he was willing to pay for it, she would oblige.

But she had never let him give her a bath.

She lolled around and lifted her legs so he could see her cunny in the water. "Do you want to soap me now?"

"Yes," he whispered.

She climbed and squatted in the smaller tub next to the first, prying loose the bar of soap that was stuck to it. She handed it to him and stayed squatting. "Go on, Mr. Henchley. Reach between my legs with the soap and lather me up. I like to be clean. Very, very clean."

He dropped to his knees upon the carpet in front of her, dipping the bar of soap in the big tub to wet it, then making a good lather with his hand. He set the soap aside and brought his fingers to her cunny, squeezing the lather into the soft, dripping curls and watching her face.

Sukey's expression softened. She had been used hard and used by many, and was unaccustomed to any gentle treatment. Her previous encounters with Henchley had been fleeting—she had pulled him off into her tight hand or he had fucked her quickly with her skirts up in the hall. Nothing to shout about. But this—she *liked* this.

He ran his hand from the front to the back of her cunny, slipping a well-soaped finger into her arsehole at the very last second and sliding it out just as quickly. Her eyes opened wide. "Now then, Mr. Henchley. Arse play costs extra too."

"How much?"

"A guinea."

"Done."

He lathered up the bar of soap and gave her cunny the same treatment, sliding a well-soaped finger into her behind just as before, leaving it in a little longer. Sukey clenched her arsehole around his finger and watched his face. His lips opened in a silent gasp as he held his finger inside as long as he could.

"That will be two guineas, Mr. Henchley." She rose up a few inches, and his finger slid out.

"Once more, if you please. You are a hot little bitch, Sukey." He lathered up for a final round, gave her cunny thorough but gentle attention, and then reached back between her legs to pop his finger into her arsehole. "You are nice and stretched." He moved it in and out. "Do you like that? Does it feel as good as the duster handle? I can just imagine how much those two men liked seeing it go up your arse."

"Yes, sir," she whispered. "I liked it too. Now and then. But you cannot fuck me there. Cunny fucking only. And that was three times you put a finger in my arse. That will be three guineas."

Henchley sighed and sat back on his haunches. His erection was at half-mast. "That is all I can afford. Time to rinse you off."

Sukey stood up in the small bath with his assistance, a little stiff from squatting for so long. She stretched out her calf muscles like a dancer—she had been a dancer once but it seemed like a very long time ago. Whoring was a more lucrative profession—so was blackmail—but both took their toll.

Henchley picked up the washcloth and floated it in the big tub, soaking it and not wringing it out. He cleaned the soap from between her legs and did not neglect her arsehole, scrubbing the tight puckers that he had stretched so gently. He squeezed out the soapy water into the small tub, soaked the washcloth again, and rinsed away every last trace of soap from between her legs.

"Lie on your back, Sukey. Spread your legs and show me your squeaky clean cunny." She obeyed, mentally adding up what he owed her: the three guineas, plus the extra for the bath play, plus the basic fee. He towered over her, his cock swelling again to its previous fullness. Then he took a giant step, turning so they would be head to tail and putting his knees on either side of her head. "Lick my balls. Suck my cock. In that order. And do it for free."

"Yes, sir." There was something in his tone that kept her from arguing. The butler let his balls brush over her face until she parted her lips and tongued them from below. Then she raised her head and gently drew most of his scrotum into her wide–open mouth—his balls were *big*. And very tasty, she thought with approval, flicking her tongue over the sensitive skin.

The inside of the tall man's thighs trembled as she kept his balls in her mouth and licked over, under, around and down. How vulnerable a man is like this, she thought. Holding very still on all fours and getting his bollocks sucked took trust.

"Ah, yes." Henchley let her lick until she gave him one final thrust of her tongue to guide him out. He used his hand to pull on his scrotum, giving a satisfied soft grunt when his balls popped out of her mouth, wet and warm. Now his hand clasped his cock and he touched the head to her lips, not able to see where to put it.

Sukey took over, guiding the throbbing rod in. He was so aroused by now that it was difficult to bend him back. She kept one hand wrapped around the shaft so he could not thrust in too far and make her splutter or cough.

He put his mouth upon her cunny, and devoured her with lips that were surprisingly soft. Then he spread her cheeks until her arsehole was revealed and quickly slid a wet finger into it. "I want you to come in my mouth while my finger is fucking you in the arse. For free."

"Yes," she panted. "All right. For free."

"I want to feel that tight hole clench when my probing tongue enters your cunny. Put your legs up over my back so I can touch you however I like." He would not tolerate her fractional hesitation. "Do it, you little bitch!"

She raised her sturdy legs and he thrust his finger all the way into her arsehole, sucking luxuriously on her drenched cunny.

Sukey moaned around his penis, rocking and pushing her crotch into his dripping face for several minutes. Then she shrieked as she felt an intense climax begin deep inside her pussy and arse, which throbbed simultaneously, one filled with a thick, wet tongue, and the other with a large finger. Henchley exploded at the same time into her mouth, releasing a full load of come, crying out with each pulsing shot.

Practice makes perfect, she thought, as she swallowed every drop without gagging. She almost never experienced orgasm herself with a customer, but she had made an exception this time. Sukey reminded herself that Henchley was only a customer.

He sat back on his haunches, her head between his thighs and gave her the cloth to wipe her mouth. She pushed it away and licked her lips instead. Then she rolled around and got up clumsily, like a little cow. "I am dirty now. I think I will have another bath, if you don't mind."

Henchley rose as well, helping her climb back into the big tub now that the sex was over and done with.

"I do enjoy the water, Mr. Henchley."

He nodded and sat down, staring into the shimmering water for a last glimpse of her cunny, getting a good look at her wet tits.

She slapped them lightly and made them bob in the water, laughing at the look on his face, then lolled for several minutes more. "I should get out or I will catch my death of cold. Give me your hand."

He didn't. His face was stony and his expression distant. The momentary tenderness and fierce sensuality between them had not lasted long. "Get out on your own, Miss Lyddington."

She gaped at him with astonishment. "How on earth did you find out my last name? No one in this house has ever used it, except—" Did she dare say *Bertie*? Her real master. Who had hired her as a real maid. All games aside, only Bertie knew her full name.

"I looked in that little book you stole. Bertie's journal."

"He gave it to me. You could not read it—it is in code," she snapped, scrambling out, not caring if she splashed, and grabbing a towel.

"Ah. Then we *are* talking about the same book."

She realized too late that she should have denied all knowledge of it.

"I found the paper that Lady Gilberte used to decipher it among your things, Sukey, today—directly after we came back from the country. In one of the bags you left for someone else to carry."

"You filthy sneak!" She looked into his eyes, which were icy and blank. "But why did you—" A sudden thought struck her. "You made me climax, Henchley. Why? You never did before."

"Not that you cared, so long as you got your money."

She wrapped the towel tightly around her naked body, as if it would protect her from the coldness in his tone. "I don't understand."

Henchley sighed, as if the answer were quite obvious. "I wanted something from you that a whore never gives. I want you to open up—to display your desire as nakedly as your body."

"You wanted to own me!" she shrieked.

He shook his head. "No. What man would truly want to own a slut from the streets? You'll be poxed and dead before you're thirty, Su. I wanted you to give yourself for free."

"I hate you!"

"Love and hate—two sides of the same thing."

She slapped him across the face and the towel fell. Sukey stood there sobbing, her bare, quivering flesh making her seem utterly vulnerable. He smiled at her like a wolf baring its fangs.

"What d'you want from me now, Hench?"

"I will get to that in due time. For now, you may kneel on the floor and pretend to be humble."

"Damn you! I shall do no such thing—" She swallowed a gasp when he slammed her to the floor and put a foot on her chest, looking up at him with eyes so wide open that the white showed all around, too afraid to wriggle free. Henchley was big enough and strong enough to break all of her ribs and smash her heart through her spine if he wanted to—and the look in his eyes told her that he just might.

"Behave, Sukey. You took the book back and hid it. Where?"

"I will tell you," she panted. "Don not press so hard upon my—chest—or my heart."

He eased the downward pressure of his foot ever so slightly. "All right. I like seeing you like this, Su. Your cunny is still pink from play and your eyes are so round and pretty."

She attempted a flirtatious tone. "I like to play rough, sir. And I can see that you are getting nice and hard. But what do you know about Bertie's book?"

He increased the force again, glaring at her with deadly calm.

"Ow!"

"I—I was only asking, Hench. The book is still in Lady Gilberte's room. I had nowhere safe to hide it when we went to the country and so I first stuck it in the jewellry drawer, which she had left open as we were packing. Then I moved it . . . elsewhere."

Henchley nodded. "I thought something like that had happened. I was standing outside her room—I heard her scold you when she caught you with your hand in the jewellry drawer."

Sukey gasped for breath.

"I had heard Lord Delamar ask Lady Gilberte a few idle questions about it when he came to see her in the country—and he said something about blackmail. She seemed to know nothing of its whereabouts and little more was said.

"Then there was Jack. I heard even more when you and he were giggling in bed. After he fucked you in your arse, where everyone likes fuck you. Where you prefer to be fucked as much as possible, because you can't get pregnant that way. Little bitch . . ." He didn't finish his sentence as he stared down at her, pressing his foot against her heart. "Jack's the one who sells secrets in the book. Takes a cut. Give you yours when he comes back for another page or two, and another go at your stretchy little arsehole. Bam. Bam. Bam. You two were at it all night.

"I could see you were jealous, Hench. But you knew I belong to no man in particular. I am only a whore."

The butler sniffed. "A whore who jumped up to the rank of lady's maid, thanks to Lord Gilberte. A devoted voyeur and scribbler of secrets."

"Yes," Sukey whispered, scarcely able to breathe.

"Secrets are lucrative. Certainly some secrets must be kept at all costs, and silence concerning them can be sold over and over again to the same buyer. Diamonds and rubies are not as valuable."

"Do—do you know which secrets those are, Hench? Did you read all of the journal?"

He shook his head and twiddled his toes between her breasts, but the life–threatening pressure of his foot was unrelenting.

"I happened to glimpse the paper with milady's notes upon its deciphering in the bag you left on the street, Sukey. You are careless. I wondered why you were carrying something with her handwriting upon it and I took it when no one was looking. Lady Gilberte is even more careless. She had written *Bertie's Journal* at the top in fine script. That made everything very easy, but I didn't have to read much before you hid it away again."

"Milady s–seems to think it is mostly lies."

Henchley stretched out his other foot and pressed it against her bare cunny. "How warm and juicy you are, Sukey girl. You and I know that much of it is true, of course. And once I pinched the paper, I knew immediately that I must find the book. Certainly it was not difficult to figure out that someone had taken it. Or who that someone was."

Sukey looked almost proud for a fleeting second, then seemed to remember that she was in danger of being stomped to death. "I will tell you where it is, then."

He leaned over her, an ominous hulk of a man with a dark light in his eyes, keeping his feet where they were. She could see his long cock hanging between his legs, the foreskin rolled over the head once more. The thought that she had pleasured that nasty thing, even held his balls within her mouth for extra licking, made her want to scream. But she held still. She had no choice.

"Thank you, Sukey. Please do."

Sukey thought with rising fury that she should have bitten off his balls when she had them in her mouth. She would *not* tell him about the second journal that Bertie had kept—and entrusted to Sukey on his deathbed. It was an obsessive chronicle of Fiona's life, rife with salacious details, and it revealed milady's most intimate secrets.

He picked up his feet, then went back into the adjoining room to put on his shirt and trousers. Sukey rolled over, drawing deep, shuddering breaths, but he spoke loudly enough for her to hear. "So now we both know how to read Bertie's journal. And we can go into business together."

"What business are you talking about, Henchley?"

"Blackmail. What else?"

12

Edward came at last a few days later and they passed an uneasy hour in each other's company. He was preoccupied and seemed troubled. Whether it had anything to do with the matters of pressing importance he had mentioned when he left Fiona at her country house, she could not tell. He certainly seemed to be thinking about something important but just what that was, he would not say.

Fiona resorted to filling the deadly gaps in the conversation with trivial talk. Edward looked irritated—with good reason, she had to admit. She disliked the artificial sound of her nonstop chatter even more than he did. Then she invited him to dinner and he refused. She attempted to converse on serious subjects and he looked out the window—at a cat stalking a pigeon, he said. And she lost her temper at last.

"Damn the cat and double damn the pigeon! Whatever is the matter with you, Edward?"

He turned from the window and looked her straight in the eye. "Fiona, I have unpleasant news. I did not know how to tell you."

"How bad can it be? Please talk to me, Edward."

He shook his head. "I find it very difficult to do so."

She looked at him narrowly. "May I have three guesses?"

"This is not a game."

She guessed anyway. "One—you are married. Two—you have fallen in love with another woman. Three—you have decided to enter a monastery . . . oh dear, that would be dreadful. For me, anyway."

"And for me as well, Fiona. Shave my head and live with men? I think not."

"Then there is hope," she said dryly. "But what is wrong? You must tell me."

He got up and paced again. She could not help but admire his fine physique. In and out of bed—or a stable—he took her breath away. Today he was dressed once more in the most elegant clothes a London gentleman could own. Buckskins. A collared linen shirt with a sober neck cloth. A light coat of dark gray superfine. Nothing fussy, nothing fancy, but his attire showed every inch of the man to advantage.

Edward clasped his hands behind his back and turned to her. "Bertie's journal is about to be published in a scandalous newspaper. In installments. Twopence a page."

"What?" Fiona sat up very straight. "But it is mostly a pack of lies, interspersed with a few good stories—which I improved upon, I might add, when I told them to you."

Edward's smile seemed forced. "You are an excellent storyteller, Fiona."

She too rose from her chair and walked about the room, too nervous to sit. "That sounds like a polite way of saying that I am a liar."

"I don't think that you are. But the great and powerful Bertrand Gilberte does."

"He is *dead*, in case the newspapers have not noticed. And he scrupulously left me out of his damned journal."

Edward nodded. "The first one, yes. He might very well have known that you'd broken the code and read it—perhaps he made the code easy to break."

"Are you insulting my intelligence as well?" Fiona asked indignantly.

"No, my dear. I am only trying to puzzle out a very odd case."

"Wait a minute. You just said something . . . about a second journal." His face was grave. "It was all about you. Where you went. Who you saw."

"And how do you know that?"

Edward looked ashamed of what he was about to say. "My valet, Jack, was given it by your maidservant. In bits and pieces."

"Sukey . . . But how did she come by it?"

"I suspect that she was being paid by your late husband to do many things."

"Not ironing and mending, you mean."

"No. She spied on you and was in an ideal position to do so."

"I thought she hated Bertie. He got her with child, the filthy old sot."

"What happened to the child, Fiona?"

"She gave it to the Coram Foundling Hospital and never saw it again. And I thought that she was grateful because I allowed her to stay on—oh, I was a fool, Edward. Most women would have sacked her. I should have done it long ago."

"Well, she kept busy watching what you did and told Bertie everything. He entertained himself by writing it all down."

Fiona sat up primly and clasped her hands in her lap. "I was not a virgin when I married him and I was no more faithful to him than he was to me."

Edward smiled a little sadly. "Well, the newspapers are going to have a field day. A friend obtained a copy of the typeset proofs, Fiona. Allow me to quote. *There are houses where rich and beautiful women go . . . where every longing is satisfied and every need is met . . . for a very dear price. My young wife has crossed the threshold of such a place . . .*" He left the last sentence unfinished.

Dear God. The other secret that she had kept from Edward had just caught up with her. She *had* been curious and she *had* gone to some of the most elegant houses of that sort. More than once. And there she had enjoyed herself with men, sensual and beautiful men, whose greatest desire was to please her.

Giving in to her considerable sexual curiosity, she had witnessed the amorous sport of women who loved only women as well. Lady Raynald was a habitué of such places, although Fiona had not found her masculine airs particularly attractive. Invited to join in, feel the soft bums of the naked and half–dressed women who pressed in upon her from all sides, or fondle a new prostitute's breasts with the female customers who'd paid for the favors of a delectable girl, Fiona had declined.

Fiona vastly preferred men, loving their gallantry, their ardor, and even their foolishness—and above all, their bodies.

She liked picking the ones she wanted and avoiding the silliness of social talk entirely. Affairs were exhausting and unpaid lovers were unreliable. At a very expensive brothel, complete satisfaction was assured.

A younger man with a big stiff rod, deferential and at her command, was all she had craved at first. She had three enjoyed at once several times, enjoying the sensation of clasping two fine cocks and riding yet another. The man on the bottom did nothing but plunge her hot cunny, while the other two took turns at fulfilling her every request. *A light spanking for my lady? Harder? Certainly. Breasts fondled by strong male hands and nipples suckled by male lips? Of course.* They had made a fine quartet.

For these sessions, she asked that her partners strip slowly, loving the shyness of the new ones as their beautiful bodies were revealed little by little. She would stroke their taut bellies and buttocks, request that the men engage in sex play to amuse her if she felt like seeing that, handling them freely as their strong hands pumped each other's cocks and slapped each other's buttocks, excited by their forbidden sport.

And she had also enjoyed trios. Fiona had particularly loved to straddle a man sitting in a chair, keeping her back to him while he held her firmly in position for the other man, who would kneel to face her and spread her nether lips gently apart to lick her to climax. It was extremely pleasurable to feel her cunny filled with a big cock, her bottom resting on muscular thighs, and big hands holding her safely, while her lover let her enjoy another man's tender tongue.

Some fellows were better for slap and tickle, rolling her around roughly in an unconcerned way, possessing an animal sexuality that never seemed to flag. One might be home in an hour, ready for a bath and bed—short romps that were wonderful for the complexion.

The more mature men, who understood a woman's ever-changing moods and helped bring her most intense, most secret fantasies to life, were even more appealing. There was no desire that seemed strange to them, no pleasure that should be denied. . . .

But she had never known that the odious Bertie contrived to spy upon her even in those hidden rooms.

"I suppose he had informants in the houses—" she stopped herself.

"What houses, Fiona?"

She fell silent.

"Never mind. I know what you are talking about."

"Of course. You have read a detailed account in the newspaper proofs."

He shook his head. "I went to such places myself, my dear. It is a wonder we never met."

"One did not mention one's last name. And the lights were low. Some wore half–masks." She smiled slightly, remembering one very lovely woman whose flowing hair was as black as the domino that concealed her identity. She had wanted to be penetrated by two men at once, riding a hard–cocked young fellow who spread her arse open for his friend to ease into her tight hole.

Fiona had looked long at the big rod in the other woman's cunny, even touched the balls of the second man, as he straddled the other woman and her lover, giving them both deep pleasure with careful strokes of his unusually long penis.

She sighed . . . a drawn–out exhalation from the bottom of her soul. Now the whole world would know how much she liked sex. Did that make her evil? No. Roses did not wilt when her shadow fell upon them and she did not keep a black cat or fly about on a broom and she had endeavored to be a kind person when and where it counted. Was that not enough?

As a very young woman, she had been as good as sold to a vile old man, given away in a nuptial rite that owed everything to hypocrisy and nothing at all to love. She had loathed Bertie and shunned his bed, finding pleasure elsewhere. Would she never be free of him? His crooked old shadow still loomed large over her life.

"If people wish to pay to read the ramblings of a cruel and selfish man, then neither you nor I can stop them. That excerpt was edited, by the way. Bertie never wrote that well." She paused. "Oh dear. Perhaps he did. I never read the second journal. Only the first."

"Nonetheless, people believe anything that appears in print. Whether the author is dead or alive makes no difference so long as there are plenty of juicy details and a few recognizable names. Like yours."

Fiona frowned. "A few weeks ago you did not know who I was, Edward. Nor did you know Bertie or he know you."

"No one knew the entire story, not even you. I have only just pieced it together."

"Then tell it to me."

"I scarcely know where to begin," he sighed.

"Anywhere."

"All right. Your Sukey was a prostitute before she became your lady's maid."

Fiona shook her head. "Why does that not surprise me?"

"Bertie paid her well to service him sexually and act out his fantasies. She played various parts, according to his desires."

"She played the skin flute best of all," Fiona said bitterly. "The little slut."

"But when Bertie died," Edward continued, "that source of income dried up. She desperately needed another. Then she found his journal—and quite by accident, your handwritten notes on its decipherment. Although it is possible that Bertie gave her both."

"Ah." Fiona sank into a chair. "I should have thrown all his papers into the fire."

"She wrote to the people whose names she found, enclosed a fair copy of his description of their sexual habits and partners, and waited for money to arrive by return post."

"How did she do?"

"Well enough. Not everyone paid, of course. But perhaps you never realized how much of Bertie's journal was true. Or should I say *true enough?*"

Fiona shot him an angry look. "You are splitting hairs. Why did Sukey stay on?"

"She signed your name to the blackmailing letters, Fiona."

So that was why she had been shunned by so many in her social class. She had not understood it at the time: her love affairs had been reasonably discreet, she had not stolen a husband that any wife wanted, and her sexual tastes were not *particularly* outré.

Fiona had thought it was due to her husband's much more unsavory reputation. Or her father's talent for losing all his money—the greatest sin of all in the eyes of the *ton.*

"I still do not know how you became involved, Edward."

"I had the whole story from Jack, my valet, just this morning. He is missing quite a few of his teeth, by the way, because he was beaten to a pulp last night by Henchley."

"Henchley? The imperturbable Henchley? What has he to do with any of this?"

"I'm coming to that. Your butler is in gaol at that moment, and will be transported when they are tired of feeding him in a year or two. Anyway, Henchley explained to Jack—mostly with his fists—that Sukey told him to thrash him—did you know that Sukey was paying my valet to extract money from the people she was blackmailing?"

"Obviously not," Fiona snapped.

"Forgive me," Edward said, shaking his head. "I did not mean to make an inadvertent accusation. But as Jack related the whole story, I began to understand that Henchley was fucking Sukey on the sly. He somehow forced her to give the first journal, which he sold to a newspaper publisher. Then Sukey produced the second, which was all about you, and—"

Fiona put her fingers to her temples. "I need a headache powder."

"My dear, so do I."

She slumped in her chair. "So I am to be pilloried in the penny papers."

"Twopenny."

"What can we do, Edward?"

"Nothing. Nothing at all. We shall have to leave the country."

We? Had he really said we? She looked at him narrowly.

"But only I am tainted by this new scandal." She laughed bitterly. "It quite puts poisoning Bertie into perspective—not that I did. However, no one cared when he died, but reputations are very different. Everyone will turn against me."

Edward came to where she sat and kneeled before her.

"To hell with them all. Live with me and be my love."

Fiona gave him a look of wide-eyed disbelief. "Where?"

"Italy," he said simply.

"Surely you are not proposing marriage."

"Of course not, darling. Most married couples loathe each other within weeks of the wedding."

Fiona nodded. "I loathed Bertie weeks *before* the wedding. I cannot pretend to be romantic about marriage, although I am sorry to say it."

Edward got up a little awkwardly. "And proposals are damned hard on the knees."

"Now who is a cynic?"

"Not I."

"How can you say that?"

He walked about the room with his hands clasped behind his back. "I am proposing a faithful union, Fiona. Though we have not known each other long, we are two of a kind and well suited. And I must own that I have loved you from the start."

"Oh," she said in a very small voice. Did she dare reveal her feelings for him? No. Not yet. She would listen to him for a change. "In what way are we so alike?"

"We are both well-born, for one thing—but wild by nature. And I think we understand each other on that score, do we not?"

"Yes. I cannot deny it. I suppose I should have told you more about myself."

"We have not spent much time talking. But I trust my instincts in such matters." He circled her chair, looking down upon her with affectionate regard. "I guessed at your experience, Fiona, from the way you made love. And the stories you told did not all come from Bertie's journal. The intimate details of those erotic scenarios were very much of a woman's devising. You are talented—very talented."

"For what it is worth."

"You captivated me, Fiona, in a very short period of time. No, I did not take you for an innocent nor did I care. Do you know, dearest, I think we have been seeking the same thing, but in very strange places."

"And what would that be?" Fiona inquired.

"Love. For all of your sexual adventuring, there is still something untouched about you, as I said."

"I suppose you mean my heart," she said slowly.

"I do."

"But you are far too wild to let yours be claimed by one woman," she burst out, rising from her chair.

"That depends upon the woman. You seem to have done it, Fiona. And even the wildest creatures sometimes mate for life."

She opened her mouth to reply and he kissed her instead.

13

Storm after storm battered the ship that sailed down the coast of Portugal, and the worst one of all blew them through the Straits of Gilbraltar. Fiona spent most of her time in their cabin, being violently ill, and Lord Delamar fared only slightly better.

Some days later, she awoke alone and struggled to dress. The floor of the cabin had ceased its wild tipping from side to side, and she knew they must have arrived in the calmer waters of the Mediterranean at last.

"Fie!" she muttered, giving up on the buttons in back and throwing on a soft Paisley shawl. They had come away with very little and she had no servants to call upon to help her. Fiona ventured above deck at last, looking for her love. And there he stood, leaning over the rail, his dark hair ruffled beyond all hope of combing it.

She patted him softly on the back. "Not vomiting again, I hope."

He turned with surprise and took her in his arms, not minding if the sailors saw or what they might think in the slightest. "Hallo Fiona! No, not at all. The air is very fine and we are running before the wind. I am told that we shall reach Florence ahead of time."

The timbers and rigging creaked pleasantly as the sails billowed out, taut from the wind and stretched to their farthest corners by it.

"How wonderful that we are here, Edward . . . and safe." She nestled into his arms, loving the strong beat of his heart against her wan cheek.

"Yes, we have seen the last of England. There is no reason to ever go back, my darling. We shall live in a warmer country, with a very different sort of people."

"What if they don't understand us?"

"All to the better, Fiona! Then we will not comprehend their criticism or suspicion. But you will see—the circles in which we will move are sophisticated indeed. The Italians are pleasure-loving people, and disinclined to judge foreigners. They simply assume we are lunatics and let it go at that."

Fiona laughed and let him hold her tighter. He slipped his hand under her shawl and happened to touch the bare flesh of her back.

"What? Not buttoned? Your dress might fly away, my lady!"

"I don't care. So long as I am with you, I am happy, Edward."

He bent his head to hers and kissed her long and lovingly . . .

Fiona dashed up the old stone stairs to the door of a tower room with a balcony. Scented herbs grew in every crevice of the words, and a profusion of little flowers with succulent leaves as well. "How kind of the contessa to lend us a castle, Edward! And how rich she must be to have one to lend!"

He caught up with her. "Her family has owned it for an eternity, probably since the days of the Romans. They are worth millions, to be sure, but I think it is all in olives."

Fiona giggled. "Carry me over the threshold, please."

"We are not married," he pointed out.

"Thank God for that."

Edward swept her up in his arms and brought her inside the room. It had been outfitted as a lovers' hideaway, hung with red silks, and a vast featherbed occupied the center of the room.

"If we must be outcasts, this is a wonderful place to do it," he said.

Fiona looked around curiously. "Is that a swing, Edward? Indoors?"

He set her down upon her feet. "I believe it is."

Fiona went to it and ran an appreciative hand over the fine velvet that upholstered it. "Such soft cloth and so thickly padded. It seems made for pleasure. One might put one's bottom precisely in the middle and swing for hours, looking out over the sea through the windows."

He gave her a wicked grin. "A naked bottom. Yours. Now that is what I would like to look at for hours. To hell with the sea. Get undressed, Fiona."

She made short work of that task, and soon stood before him, gloriously nude, and enjoying the slight breeze that made her nipples stand out so nicely. "And you?"

"I shall keep some clothes on. My breeches at least. That way I won't be tempted to possess your cunny too soon." He pulled off his coat and then his neck cloth, putting it aside, then yanking his shirt out of his breeches and wrestling it off.

"Do not rip it in your haste," she said softly. Fiona went to the swing again and pushed it a little, to and fro. Before she knew it, Edward was by her side, turning her around with his hands on her waist. He hoisted her onto the swing, belly down, but held it in place. "Oh!" she cried, kicking her legs.

"Hold still," he growled. He wrapped her shawl swiftly around her middle and the swing itself and tied the shawl over her back, then came around to tie her hands together with his neck cloth. "Kick all you want, Fiona. Show your cunny. I want to stand in back of you and see it all. I want your behind to bump my face with each backward swing while you laugh and enjoy yourself. We are free at last. And I fully intend to spend the rest of this beautiful day fucking you silly."

"Then give me a push."

He did. She swung lazily back and forth, giggling with wanton pleasure, glad to be bare. Edward watched for a few minutes, then began to stroke her buttocks each time she came back to him. On the fifth swing, he grasped them with all his strength and held her in mid–air, burying his face in her cunny.

"Uhhh . . ." She groaned with pleasure, feeling giddy from the swing and her own wanton freedom. "Put your tongue very deep in . . . ohhh . . . like that!" She let her legs and arms relax completely as he licked her from the inside out, being delightfully noisy about it and holding the swing where it was. They were literally up in the air in the tower room and Fiona might as well have been on a cloud, receiving a thorough oral pleasuring from her own personal man–angel.

He set to work and thrust his tongue all the way in. Then out. Then in. Fiona groaned again. He pulled his face and slapped her on the buttocks. "Off you go!" Edward gave the swing a strong push and ducked under and she sailed up. Now I shall watch you from the front. Just look at those tits. Right where I want them." He positioned himself so that his hand just cupped her breasts and brushed her nipples on each forward swing. Fiona felt a gathering excitement course through her body and she strained forward each time to ensure that he made contact. The delicacy of the pressure upon the very tips of her nipples, the tantalizing second or two that elapsed between its repetition, and the coming forward again to fill his strong palms, was deeply erotic.

Edward laughed with delight. "Aha! I had not realized that I can see you from the back in the mirror. Two Fionas! No man could ask for anything more. Kick your legs, darling. You look so pretty when you do. There . . . yes . . . here are your tits in my hands again . . . and there is your bottom in the mirror again . . . and a very flushed cunny. You like swinging, don't you?"

"I adore it, Edward. Do you suppose this wonderful swing was put here for this purpose?"

He rolled his eyes at that question. "Well, it was not put here to serve coffee, Fiona." He brushed her sensitive breasts again and just managed to gently and quickly pinch each nipple.

She kicked and swung back. "Untie me soon. I am quite giddy, although I like it."

He grabbed the swing's ropes on the next go, and let her down. Fiona ran to the bed and jumped in it, rolling herself up in the featherbed and rolling out again. She went about on all fours, putting the corners back in place while he tugged off his boots and then his breeches.

At the last corner, he pounced, covering her body with his and touching his erect cock to her cunny. He didn't wait and he didn't ask, just spread her pussy lips apart and rammed it in to the hilt. Pinned by the pleasure of it, Fiona stayed on her hands and knees, turning her head to respond to his murmured demand for a kiss. Their tongues tangled for a few seconds, then he bit the back of her neck and gripped her tits in hard hands.

"I need to do it this way, Fi—let me take you hard."

She moaned a yes just as he shoved himself into her again, not waiting for her answer, clasping her around the belly, then hips, moving like an animal with fast strokes that filled her completely.

"Do your cunny, love. I want to fuck and I don't care if you come. I want to—" he pulled back and almost very slowly until she could feel her nether lips clench the swollen head of his huge shaft—"I want to see how deep you can take it . . . ahhh!" He rammed his cock in like the god of thunder and kept the savage rhythm going, releasing pent–up male energy but no his seed. She put her head down upon the bed and stretched a hand back beneath her thighs to touch her pleasure bud. But his balls bounced against it and she decided to stroke him instead, feeling the sac tighten at her touch and draw up against his body. "My beautiful bitch . . . on all fours for me . . . spread and taking it . . . hard! Hot and hard!"

She felt him his thighs shake and he reared up, hanging onto her hips with all his might and pounding his cock home, spurting his hot come into her with wild cries. Then he rested upon her back, sweating and exhausted, but with enough presence of mind to not become a dead weight upon her.

The feeling of holding him up was oddly pleasant. Dreamily, Fiona touched their joined parts with gentle strokes, enjoying the silkiness of the dripping, semi–hard cock as it slipped out of her cunny and using it to rub upon her pleasure bud. He was long enough and it felt like a tongue.

His tongue.

Edward stirred and reached around to fondle her tits. All the wonderful hot sensations coursing through her body, still bracing his, gathered together into an explosive orgasm.

They collapsed together in a tangle of satisfied flesh. The last thing Fiona remembered seeing before she feel asleep in his arms was the swing, swaying slightly in the warm Mediterranean breeze.

14

Some months later . . .

Fiona stretched out upon a divan that had been placed outside in the patio to take advantage of the fine weather, very much at ease in the sun, toying with the sweet cherries in a dish at her side. She knew that Edward was watching her from the corner of his eye, though he pretended to be absorbed in an architectural treatise, so she picked up a particularly plump one and let the cherry dangle from its stem above her parted lips.

She heard him draw in an almost inaudible breath, through his eyes were fixed upon the page when she looked at him. Fiona kept the cherry where it was and touched the tip of her tongue to it. Then she sucked it into her mouth and chewed it thoughtfully, ridding her mouth discreetly of the pit.

Edward gave up pretending to read and laughed. "How sensual you are, my dear."

"Am I?" She rolled on her back and gave him an indolent look. "Then come here, you fool."

"Very well." He closed the book and crossed to her, sitting on the edge of the divan and putting one arm over her waist.

"Kiss me."

He obliged but soon sat up again.

"Is that all?"

Edward smiled slightly. "For now."

Fiona pouted just for effect. "Oh, dear. I wanted to sample every single delight that Italy affords."

"You have certainly sampled enough of those cherries. Be careful not to give yourself the bellyache. We are to journey to Don Giuseppe's villa in a day's time, do not forget."

Fiona yawned. "Oh yes. The house party. Our final fling before we settle down, or so you said. And what amusements are planned, Edward?"

He leaned over and whispered in her ear.

"Then I shall not have to pack very many clothes."

"No, my darling." They shared a conspiratorial look—and the rest of the cherries.

The villa was ancient, with far more rooms than the Mayfair mansion Fiona had sold before they fled England forever. And the company was elegant. Fiona still spoke very little Italian, but the warmth and graciousness of the guests who spoke it to her put her quite at ease. Their murmured whispers of *bella, bella* when she happened to walk by did not seem trouble Edward, who kept her on his arm, introducing her to handsome men whose eyes seemed to burn into her and the sophisticated women with them.

"So tonight is the night, then?"

"Yes," he said quietly. "If you do not like what they do, then we may leave."

"But you have been here before."

"Yes."

"And enjoyed yourself."

"Oh yes, Fiona. With many lovers. No names are exchanged and no promises are made. It is all about giving and receiving of pleasure . . . many kinds of pleasure. And you may well feel less constrained if you do not speak their language. I shall watch—and participate if you want me to."

She nodded. "I trust you."

The moon ruled the night sky, outshining the stars, by the time the varied company retired to a luxurious suite of rooms to disrobe in alcoves hung with brocades and silks for their privacy. One by one they appeared, as dressed as they wanted to be.

Fiona, wearing only a light corset that cinched her waist to a sensual narrowness, peeped out from behind a gap in their drapes. The scene was dreamlike, as men and women lolled upon divans and low chairs, being served wine and stronger drink by impassive servants dressed all in black.

But the sober color of their livery did not conceal the fact that they too had sensually beautiful bodies of every type. She remembered her late husband's careful selection of servants, and had a smile. Don Giuseppe was of the same mind, evidently.

She turned around to see that Edward was quite naked. His imposing strength and taut musculature still took her breath away. But he was not erect—yet. "Come, my lady," he said. She swallowed her nervousness, too his arm and stepped forth, hearing the same murmured word as before. *Bella.*

Without further ado, he brought her to sit by a soft-bodied woman, with shimmering black hair that fell nearly to her knees. Other than her curtain of hair, the woman was entirely naked. The warmth of the room, the wine she had consumed, and the elegant strangeness of the scene conspired to make

Fiona's head swim rather pleasantly. The woman, who she realized was not speaking Italian, took a puff from a many-armed water pipe and offered it to Fiona.

She looked at Edward, who nodded as if giving her permission. Fiona drew in a puff of the burning substance and then another, feeling her body and brain sink into a sensual languor that seized her completely. After several minutes, it seemed as if the black-haired woman was talking from a very great distance away, although Fiona knew that Edward was holding her.

His warm, lightly furred arms encircled her. Without shame, Fiona pulled up her knees and let her thighs fall open. The black-haired woman looked appreciatively between and asked Edward something.

"Say yes for me," Fiona whispered.

"I don't know what she said," he whispered back. "But I met her here last time, Fiona. She is a lover of women and a former inhabitant of a harem. And I would love to see her lick your pussy while I hold you safe. You have been to the finest brothels in London . . . but now you can share an experience from a Arabian dream . . . with me. Do you want to?"

"Yes . . . oh yes," she murmured, gazing into the woman's smoldering eyes. Edward indicated by a gallant gesture that he was willing to share his beloved and the black-haired woman kneeled between Fiona's open legs.

She looked around through heavy-lidded eyes. Similar groups—duos, trios, and quartets—were forming. Some guests preferred to remain solo and some chose an attractive servant or two for their pleasure. Two men had a completely naked woman, her white-blond hair done up with a rope of pearls, tied up with straps of black velvet so that her pale breasts stuck out more temptingly from her body. One slid his cock between her parted lips . . . the other slid his into her silky-haired blond cunny. They began to fuck her in two different places but at the same time, in the same rhythm. The sight was mesmerizing.

Fiona realized that she was moaning. Waiting for the moment of penetration for the writhing blonde, she had not noticed the Arabic woman's lips poised over her own cunny nor that she was being orally serviced with subtle skill, in a way had probably been handed down from centuries of harem odalisques. It eclipsed every such encounter she'd had in the London bordellos—no, it transcended them all.

No jostling, no sharp talk from jealous Sapphics vying for a sluttish girl . . . just intense, exquisite pleasure from another woman's mouth.

"Ohhhh . . ."

Edward loosened his grip though she could feel his gigantic rod against her back and the moisture that the pressure of her body had squeezed from the tip.

He teased her breasts until the black-haired woman raised her glistening mouth from Fiona's cunny and sat back on her haunches. She took silk threads from a tray of sexual toys and spun them in her fingers with magical swiftness, tying the light cords she made around each of Fiona's nipples in turn. Edward helped the woman unlace Fiona's corset and let her wriggle free, now entirely naked.

"You have done this before," Fiona whispered.

"Yes, my love. And I am sure you will like it."

The Arabic woman rose, tugging at the cords until Fiona cried out in the faintest of voices, surprised by the delicacy and intensity of the stimulation. The other woman gave the cords to Edward. A nearby man, standing with his muscular legs apart as he stroked his long, thick cock and observed Fiona's helpless pleasure, said something in Italian to him.

Edward translated. "The ties of pleasure are light . . . but one does not want to break them. Do you like your nipples in bondage, my darling?" He tugged on the fine cords and made the pink areolas draw up. The black-haired woman bent over and took each nipple into her mouth by turns. Just as she had done for Fiona's pussy, she sucked with consummate skill. The watching fellow moved behind her, spreading her soft buttocks completely apart. The men who had been fucking the blonde stopped to give her a rest and watch the new combination of bodies form. The beautiful blonde opened her drowsy eyes—she had been enjoying the penetrating force of two healthy men very much, judging by the blurry shape of her lips and the well-fucked fragrance of her cunt—and focused on Fiona.

The Arab beauty's lover gathered up her silken waterfall of hair and held it to one side, the better to reveal her private parts to everyone in the room. She began to undulate her hips, moaning and singing softly in the keening voice of a woman near orgasm, mimicking the motions of climax with sensual rolls and bends. Her breasts touched Fiona's face and body as she moved. Then she clasped Fiona's spread thighs and waited to be entered by her man, who pumped a few drops of come onto her smooth buttocks, releasing a little to enable himself to last longer, poising himself between her shaved nether lips when he was ready.

The Arab beauty swung her hips faster. A passing woman bent down to lick up the drops from the black-haired woman's behind and gave him an encouraging slap on his arse. The man thrust in deeply without further ado.

Fiona felt Edward lift her easily and settle her higher on his body. His cock was just below her cunny, his legs spread just like hers and supporting hers. The black-haired woman helped him position his swollen member to enter Fiona but Fiona needed no help from anyone. She slid down upon his shaft herself, over and over, filling herself completely.

Her Arabian lover bent forward and applied her odalisque's skills to Fiona's cunny, fingering her clitoris and pulling on the slick little bud. Edward, who had been handed the fine cords wrapped around Fiona's nipples, tugged at them once more. Fiona climaxed, screaming with excitement so deep it seemed it would never end, could never end . . . and melted in his arms.

15

Fiona opened her eyes and looked around to find that she still reclined on the divan, but Edward no longer lay underneath her. He had moved to one side on the capacious divan, his huge cock lost inside the Arabian beauty's mouth, his hand tangled in her black waterfall of hair.

Curious—deeply curious—to see how this expert in oral pleasure stimulated her lover, Fiona leaned closer to watch. Edward's swollen member pulsed each time the Arab woman wrapped her lips around it. He tightened his buttocks to push up and into her mouth more deeply, watching her tease the underside with rapid flicks and vibrating moans each time he fell back upon the soft cushions.

The man who had been fucking her stopped, keeping his hand on her hips so she was braced against him, her head down in Edward's tense groin, her hair flowing over his thighs and belly. He cast a sideways glance at Fiona.

"Do you like to watch, my love? You are not jealous . . . ?" he moaned involuntarily as the Arabian beauty sucked him harder "... I was not jealous when she licked your cunny with such lascivious care . . ." He drifted away again for a few blissful seconds and then reached out a hand to touch Fiona's flushed face. "Your eyes are glowing."

She pressed her check into his palm. "How could I be jealous?" she murmured. "I like to watch. You know I do. And she is giving you so much pleasure."

The Arabian beauty pulled away from him for a moment, her reddened lips slick and full. She leaned over Edward's prone body, resting her breasts on his taut belly and kissed Fiona full on the mouth.

Fiona opened her lips, enjoying the mingled flavor of Edward's sucked cock, her own pussy juices, and the Arab woman's mouth, fragrant with a light, unfamiliar spiciness that tasted like the very essence of sex.

The black-haired woman slid her fingers through Fiona's tumbled hair, deepening the kiss as Edward watched, grasping his slick cock and pumping in gently with her free hand.

She broke off the kiss and indicated that Fiona was welcome to take a turn with the cock she grasped. Fiona nodded and bent her head over Edward's groin, taking the hot, empurpled head between her lips and licking it all around. The Arab woman held his penis firmly, keeping the foreskin withdrawn but using it to rub and stimulate the topmost part of Edward's thick shaft.

Seeing two woman so intent upon his member made Edward hold very still. He spread his thighs wide apart to give them more room. The Arab woman took Fiona's hand and let her clasp him, while she applied her lush mouth to his balls, licking and nipping at the heavy sacs.

The man behind her began to thrust again, very excited by the sight. Others gathered around to watch, mostly men, who put their hands around their own members and stroked themselves.

A young servant, a man of twenty with a slight build, his clothes long since removed, got upon all fours and showed his behind, awaiting a taker. He did not have long to wait. An older man soon knelt in back of him and anointed his arsehole with a dab of thick unguent from a tray by the divan and thrust in deeply, reaching around to cup the young servant's testicles and stroke his cock.

A very pretty woman came over to watch this sport and knelt beside the two men, caressing the young servant's fair hair and exclaiming in Italian over his beauty. He put his head in her lap, letting her stroke his hair while the man behind him took full advantage of this shift in position and thrust ever deeper into the young man's arsehole.

Fiona watched them, fascinated, but continued to suck Edward's cock, sliding her hand up and down the shaft. The pretty woman looked up at her and smiled, then looked down again at the young servant, whose face rested on her silken thighs, which he kissed.

The man behind pulled out. He indicated that he wanted the young servant to fuck the woman, who seemed to be his mistress, and she lay back upon the carpet, clasping her bent legs behind her knees and spreading completely open. The watching men stroked their throbbing rods faster, staring at each other now and then but most of all at the trio of shameless lovers on the thickly carpeted floor.

Then the young servant got on top of her, lying down blissfully in her encircling arms and moving his cock in a sensual but very slight side to side motion that made her moan. Yet, knowing what was expected of her, the woman on the floor spread her buttocks with eager hands. The other man prepared himself to mount them both, adding more unguent to the arsehole he had just been fucking with such pleasure. He kept himself up with one arm, deftly inserting his penis into the tender behind that his mistress held open for him, then put both hands on the floor, moving in and out of the young man with long strokes.

The double rhythm and the deep pounding made the pretty woman cry out with pleasure, and as she began to come, the young man in the middle did too. The older man wielded his cock expertly, ramming himself up the hilt in the servant's arse, and reaching climax at nearly the same time. The men gathered round soon began to ejaculate as well, a fountain of long, overheated, spurting cocks in a half–circle.

The Arabian beauty threw back her hair and laughed with sensual joy. She moved her hips in the strange, undulating motion that Fiona had observed before, giving herself fully to the man who was still fucking her from behind until he too cried out and came with long, shuddering breaths.

She waved him away when he was done, tucking a soft linen cloth between her legs to soak up the trickle of jiz, and returning her attention to Edward, who was still stiff with desire. The muscles of his belly and chest stood out, hard and shapely, as he clutched the edge of the divan with his hands.

Ah, yes. There was that iron cock and iron self–control, Fiona thought, feeling a surge of love for him. How wonderful it would be to see him come at the very last, arching his back and crying out helplessly, half–mad with pleasure.

The onlookers had drifted away and the sensual trio of two men and their lady had risen to enter the baths in the next room. Fiona had just glimpsed the *bagnio,* where still more beautiful servants of both sexes waited to refresh and cleanse the bodies of the orgy's participants, allowing them to renew their desire for still more pleasure.

Only she and the Arab woman remained by the divan where Edward lay. A shadow, its edges moving from the candlelight that illumined the hall of pleasure, fell across his naked body.

Fiona looked up. It was the pale blond woman, who had been tied up to service two men at once.

The blonde smiled shyly and rubbed her wrists where the velvet straps had been, looking down at all three of them. Fiona and the Arab woman exchanged a look, understanding each other without a word being spoken.

They assisted Edward to his feet, guiding the blonde into his arms, where she curled submissively against him. His erection bumped her white belly, spilling a few drops of seed, which she swept up with a fingertip, brought to her lips . . . then put her finger in Fiona's mouth.

The blonde and Fiona shared a kiss under Edward's heavy–lidded gaze as his hands moved restlessly over their breasts, fondling both of them. Then the Arab woman pulled the blonde gently away, leaving Fiona in Edward's embrace. He swayed a little on his feet, the only one who had not released his pent–up lust, but judging by the angle of his incredibly stiff cock and the pearly fluid that beaded its head, he was very close to orgasm.

The Arab beauty stroked the other woman's white skin, pinching her soft behind to stimulate her and make her ready for the pleasure she had in mind. She made the blonde kneel upon the divan, slapping her thighs apart. From this direction, her golden-fringed, pink–lipped cunny was fully visible and irresistibly succulent. Edward looked at her but clasped Fiona to him, murmuring something she could not hear into her hair.

She turned to see the Arabian woman select a very long dildo from another tray that hung from twisted cords around the neck of a waiting maidservant. The blonde's eyes widened when she saw it and Fiona realized that she probably did not know where it would go.

But since it was her particular pleasure to be used as anyone might wish, she made no protest, merely resting her head upon a pillow and thrusting her arse higher for all to see.

The Arab woman stuck two fingers in the blonde's silky cunny, then pulled them out with a sucking sound and wiped her hand upon the submissive woman's buttocks, inserting the dildo all the way up inside her. She smiled when the other woman's eyes widened and rammed it in another inch.

"But it is only half–in and half–out," Fiona whispered. "And much too long for one woman to take in in its entirety."

"Just watch," Edward said, looking appreciatively at the sight of the huge dildo hanging out of the blonde's cunny. "It is exactly right for two."

The Arabian woman turned around and got on the divan, arse to arse with the other woman, quickly grasping the dildo before their buttocks touched and putting the head of the thing in her cunny. Then she thrust back until her behind bumped the other woman's, who braced herself against the divan.

Rocking back and forth, slamming their soft arses together, sharing the large dildo in their hungry cunnies, the women communicated in moans and satisfied little grunts. Such play without penetration was extremely stimulating to watch, especially as the black–haired beauty rolled her hips in the same sensual way as before, rubbing her buttocks against the other woman's with utter abandon. Fiona wondered if there was no unusual pleasure the Arabian woman did not know.

She let go of Edward as the Arab beckoned him over, pulling his cock into her mouth and sucking him with her forward moves, then sliding tight lips over the shaft with the backward thrusts against the blonde's arse.

The blonde cast a come-hither look over her shoulder at Fiona. Well . . . when in Rome, Fiona thought lightly. She rested on hand upon the woman's pale back just touching the fine sheen of sweat and running a fingertip down the other woman's spine. The blonde shuddered.

Fiona moved her hand down over her white buttocks, waiting for an opportunity to get two middle fingers around the shaft the women on the divan worked between them, relishing the sensation of two fine pairs of buttocks trapping her hand, then releasing it, then trapping it again.

Edward watched her tensely, almost indifferent to the Arabian woman sucking his cock and seeming far more aroused by the flushed excitement in her eyes. "Two cunnies, Fiona, in your pretty hand . . . two luscious behinds, rubbing and rubbing . . . does it feel good to see women behave so shamelessly?"

"Yes" she whispered. "I want to feel what they are feeling. I want you to watch me share a dildo of such prodigious size with one of these women. You pick, Edward."

He grasped the Arab woman's flowing hair and pulled her mouth off his swollen cock. "Very good, my beauty. And you shall have more later. But now my lady wants to play and I want you to do the honors."

She seemed to understand, and kicked the blonde's thighs gently to get her to move forward off the dildo while she hung on to it to keep it in. The big thing, its other half slick with the blonde's pussy juices, stuck out of the Arab woman's cunny. She swayed and rolled her hips with it in, making it swing in midair for Fiona's amusement.

Edward assisted her to take the blond woman's place on the divan, putting the head of the dildo between Fiona's nether lips when she was rump to rump with—but not touching—the Arabian.

"Push yourself onto it," he said, keeping a firm hand on Fiona's bare buttocks. "It will give her pleasure when you do. Go!"

Fiona thrust back, feeling a surge of pleasure as her flesh met a very womanly behind. The Arabian beauty rubbed herself against Fiona, pushing the dildo further into both of them. The sensation of the stimulating play made her weak and she was glad she was on hands and knees.

Edward pushed the blonde to the floor beside her, and then

made her lie back with her mouth under Fiona's bobbing breasts. Fiona felt her delicate lips suckle upon one nipple, while her hand teased the other, then switch. She could just see Edward, watching with avid interest.

"A raven-haired lover pressing her soft arse into yours . . . and a blond angel doing your nipples, Fiona . . . and you, sweet as honey . . . just taking it . . . taking that big rod from one and giving your breasts to another . . ."

She was too lost in the incredibly erotic sensations coursing through her body to notice that he was spurting uncontrollably onto the blonde's belly. But he never lost sight of her.

Edward put a hand upon her cunny as Fiona was pleasured by her two partners and touched her dripping clit with light strokes. She cried out . . . then she screamed. Then she thrust backward very rapidly against the Arabian beauty's accommodating arse, coming in Edward's strong hand as his last spurts bedewed the blonde's soft belly.

The black–haired woman reached climax only seconds later, crying out in melodious words that Fiona barely heard. She pulled away from Fiona, and their pulsing cunnies released the huge dildo simultaneously. Edward stood to sweep Fiona up in his arms, making her feel as if she were held in the arms of a heroic statue of warm, living marble, looking down at the scene below.

The blonde wriggled backwards onto the divan, reaching out her arms to the Arabian beauty, begging for satisfaction. She raised her white legs up sticking her finger into her arsehole to stretch it, not caring who saw her, consumed with intense sexual need. Expertly and quickly, the black–haired bent the dildo, sliding one tip onto the blonde's cunny and the other tip into her arsehole, grasping the center to control the thrust and give maximum pleasure to its willing recipient.

The blonde moaned with joy, touching her clit, her white, pink–tipped breasts bouncing as she convulsed in a powerful orgasm. Spent, she lay back, letting the black–haired woman withdraw the dildo with care. The two women nestled in each other's arms, kissing tenderly in the afterglow of their shared sensuality . . . and Fiona looked up at Edward.

Truly, he had introduced her to a world of pleasure she had never imagined existed . . . and she craved more. She whispered her desire into his ear but Edward shook his head.

16

"No more, my love."

"But—"

Edward brought her to the *bagnio* instead. Pushing aside the heavy curtains of striped silk with one shoulder, he walked carefully over the tiled floor to the shimmering pool, a relic of the days when Don Giuseppe's villa had been owned by a wealthy Roman senator, fed by a thermal spring of hot, pure water. She kept her arms wrapped around his neck as he cradled her in his arms, nuzzling her fondly. A few other people looked up lazily, already lolling in the water but still some distance away. A few others were stretched out upon luxuriously padded tables, enjoying massages with fragrant oil.

He paused as a female servant approached, clad in white linen from head to toe and carrying a basket of steaming towels. She said something in Italian that sounded exceedingly polite, and Edward nodded to her. Without further ado, the woman slipped a towel between Fiona's crossed legs, startling her by scrubbing intimately at her stimulated flesh.

Edward grinned at Fiona's indignant expression. "The *bagnio* is shared. It's only fair."

The bath attendant finished with Fiona and unrolled a new towel to briskly cleanse Edward's cock and balls. Fiona laughed when he flinched at the attendant's amiable roughness. "So you don't like it either. Serves you right."

"Thank you for your sympathy, my darling," he answered back. "I suppose it does serve me right."

Finished with her task, the remorseless attendant moved away. Edward twirled around with Fiona in his arms. "Feeling livelier?"

"Not yet," she replied.

He stepped onto the broad, mosaic-patterned stairs that showed clearly under the water until his feet touched the bottom of the *bagnio*, then pushed on slowly, step by step, somewhat hampered by having her in his arms.

Fiona felt the warm water lap against her bottom and kicked her feet in it with delight, still clasping him by the neck.

"Ah. It does feel good." The water had reached his private parts before hers, of course. He moved in deeper, letting her down into the delicious warmth of it little by little. Fiona slid down his body and took her time about it.

The sexual pleasures they had witnessed and shared, the consummation of the powerful desires the scene and its participants had evoked, and most of all the languor induced by the naturally heated water made Fiona's excitement ebb away.

"How thoughtful of Don Guiseppe." She swam a few strokes, then rolled onto her back. "We must thank him before we leave."

"How very English of you, Fiona," he laughed.

Standing in the water, Edward was a colossus from the waist up and a very small man from the waist down. The distortion made her smile. She swam to him and clasped his private parts playfully.

"You are a very naughty mermaid. But these waters are full of them."

"Am I so very naughty? I have you to thank for leading me down the garden path, my lord."

He put a hand to his chin and thought that over. "Strictly speaking, I don't think that mermaids can navigate garden paths. Their tails, you see—very tricky—" He dove under the water with amazing speed and got her by the ankles, yanking her under.

Fiona kicked free and surfaced, splashing him when he came up. He took her in his arms once more and kissed her, wet as she was, her honey-colored hair dripping rivulets over her shoulders.

"Ah, you are lovely this way . . . the water running down your velvet skin, and your eyes . . . still on fire. I think now that I want you all to myself."

She thought again of the men in the other room. Naked or clothed, none of them compared to Edward.

"But am I enough for you?" she wondered aloud.

"My greatest pleasure is watching your pleasure, Fiona. I would not seek out tonight's company, stimulating as it is, for any other reason."

"But you have before. Oh dear," she said laughing a little. "You are very solemn for a naked man. It is difficult to take you seriously."

"I was younger then. And I had not met you. But I will admit to liking the freedom to enjoy every physical sensation," he said unabashedly.

"I must own that I do as well." Fiona shivered.

He put an arm around her shoulders. "Let us leave."

"May I retrieve my clothes?"

He craned his neck to peer into the adjacent room, where their fellow hedonists could just be glimpsed. "I believe someone else is wearing the corset you discarded."

"A woman or a man?"

Edward looked again. "A woman."

"Then she is welcome it. Unless you like the way she looks in it."

He shrugged, walking with her to the mosaic stairs at the edge of the bagnio and helping her out. Another attendant rushed forward with robes and towels. Further conversation was halted by the difficulty of dressing in haste, and the necessity of sneaking out a side portal, since most of the other revelers were in full cry and hot pursuit of new arrivals.

Their carriage was not far. The night air cooled their overheated nerves as they walked to it, muffled in hooded cloaks that none might mark their identity as guests of the notorious Don Giuseppe.

"We might invite the Arabian beauty to a party of our own someday, my love," Fiona said softly. "She is indeed a creature from a fantasy. Made to excite carnal lust and satisfy it in a thousand ways."

"If you wish," he replied, "then someday we will. She gave you very great pleasure. But no men. Just us three."

"And why no other men? Is that quite fair?"

He stopped and drew her into his strong embrace. "Because you belong to me now. Do you want another man?"

"No," she whispered. "But I want to make love again."

"As do I. But only to you this time." He brushed a wayward lock of hair back from her forehead. "Only you. Your every desire is mine to fulfill, Fiona . . . now and forever. Is that enough for you?"

"Yes, my love. Oh, yes."

What you want . . . how you want it.
THE HARD STUFF,
supersexy contemporary erotica with action that doesn't quit. Look for it. From Kensington . . .

"Who said size doesn't matter?" Stevie asked.

Must have been a little man with a little . . .

She whistled admiringly at the package, grateful for the unexpected perk.

Grinning, she dragged her eyes for a breathless second from the high-powered telescope and looked over her shoulder. The last thing she wanted was for one of the task force guys her lieutenant insisted on saddling her with to think she was some hard-up sexpot.

She laughed out loud. Okay, maybe she was. It had been too long since she last felt the sinful pressure of a man between her legs. And it wasn't because she was a prude. Unfortunately, the most intriguing prospects were the same ones she'd sworn off for years. Cops.

She'd learned the hard way not to be the company inkwell. Too many hassles. Too many knowing grins from her fellow officers, followed by suggestive wolf whistles.

Nope, she made damn sure she wasn't the hot topic of any

lineup. Besides, since her promotion to detective two years ago, she didn't have time for a relationship anyway.

She shrugged and focused back on her subject.

Mario Vincente Spoltori, aka Rocky. Not an original alias, but hell, the man was a walking hard-on. And she bet he gave granite a run for its money.

She'd been surveilling the *escort* for nearly a week, and finally after tedious hours of watching the paint dry, she got her first look at what the privileged ladies of Sacramento couldn't get enough of.

And mamma mia, there was plenty to go around.

She couldn't blame the ladies who waited months to get an hour of this notorious stud's time. No more than she could help that familiar tingle between her legs. Not for Mario. As delightful as she was sure he was in the sack, she was more straight-laced. One-nighters weren't something she actively pursued. She'd only had one in her life, and although it was the best sex she'd ever had, and she would have followed the guy to the ends of the earth, the whole experience left her feeling . . . well, tawdry.

He never called.

No use thinking about a guy she'd never see again.

Prick.

Shaking her head, Stevie gave rock-hard Rocky her full attention, and for a minute put aside the fact he was the reason she'd worked round the clock for the last three months.

She laughed and thought how ironic her current predicament was. Here she was, a perfectly healthy female, and she was considering paying for stud service. Her life was too hectic for anything less than the occasional quickie. And as picky as she was, her options were severely limited.

Strictly as a woman to his man, Stevie considered Rocky's slick muscles and generous endowment. She sighed. Too bad she wasn't into this kind of stuff.

He bent over, flexing his taut ass at her, and continued the slow slide of his underwear down his thighs before he kicked them off.

Well . . . *maybe* . . . nah. Besides, on her cop salary she'd have to give up a lot of somethings for a roll in the hay with the likes of the Italian Stallion across the way.

"Oh, you selfish bastard."

What a waste. Looked like Adonis was sneaking some of the goodies. As big as his cock was, his hand was larger. He stood stark naked facing her in front of his exposed window and stared across the wide boulevard that separated their respective buildings.

He smirked, closed his eyes, tilted his head back, and put on a show. If she didn't know better, she'd swear he knew he had an audience.

Impossible. While his windows were transparent, the small, stuffy office she'd begun to detest had a dark film covering the window, with just a small square cut out for her ever-watchful eyes. No way could he know he was under surveillance.

Stevie dismissed that thought and instead zeroed her attention back on what God had so benevolently given the man. His long dark fingers grasped his rod and in a slow pump he manipulated it to staggering proportions. Stevie licked her dry lips.

Jesus.

His hips ground against an imaginary pussy and he bit at his bottom lip.

Faster and faster and faster he pumped. Stevie's breath held when he splayed himself up against the window, still pumping. Her skin warmed. She didn't want to get sucked in by his erotic display, but she did nonetheless.

She screamed and about jumped out of her skin when the pressure of a large hand squeezed her shoulder.

"Am I interrupting?"

Her shock caused her to lose her balance and fall backward

off her chair. As she was trying to catch herself, two large, very capable hands grabbed her. The touch sent shock waves through her body. She had the undeniable inclination to rub herself up against the hard thigh that supported her back.

"Christ, what the hell?" she yelled, collecting herself and sitting up. Quickly she twisted around and pulled her piece.

She felt the blood drain from her face.

Son of a bitch.

"Jack Thornton."

"It's been a long time, Detective Cavanaugh." His grin rivaled a wide-open barn door. He seemed taller, more muscled. The faint smile lines at the corners of his deep-set hazel eyes accentuated his natural mischievous nature.

She braced herself.

Humiliation and excitement riveted through her, running neck and neck for the finish line. Her skin flushed hot and she resisted the urge to lick her dry lips.

Instead, she did what any woman scorned would do. She slapped him. Hard. White imprints of her fingers stood boldly out against the tan of his cheek. Before her hand returned home, he grabbed it. He yanked her hard against him, the connection forcing her breath from her chest. Her sensitive nipples stiffened against the hardness of his chest.

"Was that because I didn't call you or because I wouldn't let you get on top?"

Visions of their sweaty, naked bodies writhing in passion amongst the twisted sheets in her academy dorm room sprang to mind. Jack Thornton could give Rocky across the way a few lessons in pleasing a woman. Her chest tightened while other emotions she chose to ignore vied for playtime.

Stevie's breath hitched high in her throat. "That was because you're an egotistical bastard." She pushed hard against him. He released her. She holstered her Sig.

Thorn continued to grin, but the harsh glare of his eyes belied his mirth. "What's so egotistical about making love to a beautiful woman?"

Despite the warmth of the room, her nipples stood at full mast. Stevie pulled on her jacket. The last thing she wanted was to give his inquiring eyes a show.

"More like seducing a virgin."

Thorn moved in closer. "That was your choice, Stevie, not mine." He grinned like an idiot. "By the way, thanks for picking me."

After so many years, the shock of seeing the only man she'd ever had feelings for forced her off balance. The sensation left her angry, and scared.

He backed up at her fist.

"Go ahead, dickhead," she said, "keep the BS coming, I don't need more of an excuse to nail you."

"I need less of one to nail you." He stepped forward, his face a happy place. "Since we're both in agreement, what do you say, my place after we're done here?"

"Pig."

"Pride in Grace, don't I know it."

Stevie couldn't believe it. The only guy she'd dreamed about stood in front of her more than willing to go back down that seductive road with her. If her pride weren't at stake, and her heart unwilling to get squashed again, she'd have her running shoes on.

"What are you doing here?"

Casually he walked past her and looked out the tinted window. He gave the long expanse of buildings quiet contemplation. As if he'd just come back from a coffee break, he righted the tipped-over chair, then sat down and focused in across the way.

"Hmm, looks like the Italian Stallion over there needs clean up on aisle nine."

Regaining her composure, Stevie swung the lens from him,

and squatting level with it, she zeroed in herself. Geez, Rocky had his chum all over the window. "I swear, you guys just love to spread that stuff around, don't you?"

Thorn pulled the lens his way and refocused. "Yeah, it's what we do. Men hunt and propagate the species, women nurture and gather. Basic."

Stevie's eyes narrowed. Neanderthal. She'd been too starry-eyed to see it in the academy seven years ago; at least *she'd* evolved since then.

She pulled the lens back her way and focused on Rocky. "That's it, clean up your mess," she said to the gigolo. Then, as if to herself, she said, "I wonder if there was some kind of statute back then about instructors fraternizing with students?"

Thorn leaned in behind her. "No." His hot breath against her ear stirred up old familiar heat. His clean, woodsy scent engulfed her. Her blood thickened in her veins and whatever hormones she had that induced sex surged through her body. She clenched her muscles before they turned to warm mush.

Stevie remembered how she couldn't wait for her defensive tactics classes. Sergeant Jack Thornton was the instructor, and she repeatedly paid with bruises to be his test dummy.

She almost laughed. She'd had such a crush on him from the get-go. Little did she know she'd end up his parting gift.

"How's the wife and kid?"

He pulled away. "You know my divorce was final before graduation." His eyes clouded. "My stepson is with his father."

Stevie inhaled a deep breath and slowly exhaled. She didn't give a rat's ass about his home life.

"What are you doing here, Thorn?"

He grinned and stood back from the telescope. Casually he pulled back his Italian-cut suit and said, "Special Agent Thornton at your service, ma'am."

She hissed in a long breath, giving him a sideways glare. So the rumors were true. He'd dumped her for Quantico. "You damned feds, why the hell can't you leave us locals alone? Go fight your own crime."

She turned away from him, settled back on the chair he'd vacated, and refocused on Studly. "Now you made me lose him. Get out of here."

"Sorry, detective, your crime has become our crime. We're taking over from here."

"That's a crock, Thornton. Me and my men have been working this case around the clock since the first body showed up. County is coming in to help out, and I'm lead dick." She smiled tightly, keeping her eyes focused on Spoltori. "You've been misinformed."

When there was no response from him, she looked up to find him staring down at her. His eyes narrowed and a slow tic worked his right jawline. "I'm not going to get into a pissing match with you, Cavanaugh. Your chief requested we come in. We're here, I'm heading up the task force."

Stevie sprang out of the chair, throwing her shoulders back. Her antagonism mushroomed when he chuckled and said, "You've been assigned to tag along for the ride." He lowered his voice as if there were others in the room who had no business listening in on their conversation. "And, Stevie, I promise you a helluva ride."

Fury infiltrated every cell she possessed. She worked her fists open and closed. "You've got a hell of a lot of nerve coming in here, telling me you're taking over my case and then propositioning me. Do you think so damned much of yourself or so little of me?"

Thorn's wide-eyed reaction gave her a modicum of satisfaction. He quickly recovered. "I'm sorry if I've given you the impression I have no respect for you, detective." He grinned. "I think I can say with some accuracy you're one of the best cops out there. You should be, I trained you."

"You trained me all right." The words escaped before she

could call them back. He not only mentored her in the classroom and spent countless hours coaching her on the shooting range and defensive tactics, but he taught her how to ride out an orgasm for maximum satisfaction among other sexy little tricks. She squashed the memories and the heat that accompanied them.

Never bashful, she gave her one-night stand a long discriminating look. She would never admit she liked what she saw. He was taller than her five-eight by a good half a foot. His shoulders looked like a linebacker's, built into a rock-hard chest that tapered down to a washboard belly and further to a package that never reclined. The guy had the stamina of a prize bull.

She snorted in contempt. "You taught me my biggest life lesson to date." She traced a finger down his silk tie. "Trust no one." She stepped back and added, "By the way, I don't go for carnie rides."

His full lips slid into a tantalizing smile. His long tanned fingers slid into his trouser pockets. "Anytime you change your mind, detective, let me know."

"Don't hold your breath. You'll suffocate if you do."

She turned back to Rocky. He'd disappeared. Probably into the shower. Their guy had an unhealthy fixation with showerheads.

Thorn pulled up the only other piece of furniture in the empty office. A straight-back chair.

"Look, Stevie, I took this case on to work with you, not against you."

Her gut clenched. "You knew this was my case?"

He nodded. "I always do my homework. Tell you what, you can keep your people, but understand they'll have to get along with mine."

Her anger flashed. This was her case, damn it! She'd be damned if she'd just step aside.

"C'mon, detective, show me yours and I'll show you mine," Thorn offered.

Stevie grunted and, knowing he wanted to trade information, she gave him something else. She pulled her Sig. "Mine's loaded."

He smiled again, his white teeth gleaming in the filtered afternoon light. "Mine's bigger." He pulled a mini assault pistol from his shoulder holster.

Stevie whistled. "Nice piece." Replacing her weapon, she reached out her hand, palm up. "Can I touch it?"

His grin turned lethal. He handed her the weapon, his fingertips brushing her palm. Stevie ignored the warm flush the contact instigated.

"Be careful, it's cocked and will discharge at the slightest provocation."

Stevie ignored him, and ran her fingers along the smooth cold steel. She wanted one.

"The magazine holds twenty-two rounds and can discharge the whole wad in less than two seconds."

Her eyes met his. A flash of heat speared her pussy. "What's the fun in that?"

He reached out his hand and slowly withdrew the pistol, the short barrel sliding against her moist palm. In a quick movement he ejected the magazine and replaced it with another one he pulled from his jacket pocket. "Lots. It's ready for firing in less time than it takes to clean up from the first barrage."

Stevie ignored the warm wetness between her thighs and the way his nostrils flared like a dog sniffing its mate's sex.

She recognized trouble when she met it. She couldn't do this. "I'll pack up and leave you and Studly to get to know each other."

She bent down to pick up her backpack, but he grabbed her arm and pulled her up and against him. The palpable tension jolted them both. "You're not going anywhere, detective. You know this guy better than his mother. You're stuck with me."

She yanked her arm.

"Take it up with your lui if you have a problem."

A rill of frustration swept through her. The last thing she wanted was to spend her days in this stuffy office across the street from a serial killing man–whore, and watch the guy do half of Sacramento's political wives, with her ex-lover breathing down her neck. She glanced at the three photos of the lifeless victims she'd tacked up on the wall, a constant reminder of why she was there. Her gut somersaulted.

She could do this with her own people, she was a proven detective. But now? With Thorn as a constant distraction? She scowled. No way.

"Sorry to burst your bubble, but I'll quit before I'd hole up with you eight hours a day waiting to get a lead on Romeo over there."

His eyes narrowed, their gold-green irises flaring jade. "I thought you were better trained than that, detective. Can't stand a little heat? What the hell kind of cop are you anyway?"

That did it. She went toe to toe with him. In the breath of a second she was in his face, her chin notched high, her eyelids narrowed, her back stiffened. "The kind that has some integrity and doesn't have to put up with a sex-crazed fed."

"Chicken."

"Taunting me won't get you a thing, Thorn. I don't *have to* work with you. I *won't* work with you. I'd rather spend the day with Lothario over there and take my chances. At least with him I won't have to play games."

He laughed deeply. "I don't play games, detective. I play for real." He leaned into her, his face only a few inches from hers. She could see the golden flecks in his eyes and smell the minty warmth of his breath. "That guy is connected to three dead women, and I aim to nab him before he does another one. Take another look at those faces, detective." He pointed at the wall of death.

Dead eyes stared at her, begging to be put to rest.

"*I'd* work with the Wicked Witch of the West if it would bring the victims justice."

Her fists clenched and unclenched. Damn him! "My responsibility is also to the victims. But how the hell am I supposed to do my job with you breathing down my neck like a dog denied?"

"Consider it an adverse condition and deal with it."

Stevie growled. As much as she didn't want to work with Thorn she wanted to nail Spoltori more. She had a responsibility to the families of the victims and to the victims themselves. No one deserved to die the way those women had. She smiled blithely. Not even Jack Thornton.

"I'll work with you, *Jack*. But let's get a few facts straight first. You touch me, I punch you." She grabbed a handful of her breasts. She smiled inwardly at his sharp intake of breath. "These are mine. I only share if I want to. Touch them and I'll geld you."

Thorn laughed, the sound deep and mellow. "Oh, Stevie, I wish I'd had another day to spend with you."

She stepped back, sliding her hands into her jeans pockets. How many times through her haze of anger when she discovered him gone had she wished for the same thing?

"Yeah, me too. It would have taken me no time to skin you alive."

She was spared Thorn's response when another suit walked in. She deduced before Thorn's intro he was another fed.

"Detective Cavanaugh, meet Agent Deavers. He's my communications specialist."

Stevie extended her hand to the tall, handsome agent. "I'd say I'm glad to meet you, Deavers, but under the circumstances I'm feeling a little bit cheated."

He nodded and gave Thorn a knowing look. "We get that a lot."

Stevie gave Thorn a hard look. "We're already set up in my office, what do you say we use that as HQ for our party?"

Both men nodded, and it was a small consolation.

Take a walk on the wildest side of all . . . with
WOLF TALES
by Kate Douglas.
Thrilling erotica from Kensington . . .

Warmth. The most wonderful sense of warmth, of contentment. Sighing, Xandi snuggled deeper into the blankets, aware of a slight tingling in her toes and fingers, a sense of heat radiating all around her, of weight and comfort and safety.

And something very large, very long, very solid, wedged tightly between her bare buttocks, following the crease of her labia and resting hot and hard against her clit. She blinked, opened her eyes wide, saw only darkness.

Awake now, she felt soft breath tickling the back of her neck, warm arms encircling her, a hard, muscular body enfolding hers. She held herself very still, forcing her fuzzy mind into a clarity it really wasn't ready for. Okay . . . she remembered being been lost in a snowstorm, remembered thinking about building a shelter, remembered . . . nothing. Nothing beyond the sense that it was too late, she was too cold . . . then nothing.

The body behind her shifted. The huge cock—at least that much she recognized—slipped against her clit as the person holding her thrust his hips just a bit closer to hers.

Xandi cleared her throat. Whoever held her had obviously

saved her life. Everyone knew more heat was given off by naked bodies, but she'd never really thought of the concept of awakening in the dark, wrapped securely together with a totally unknown naked body. No, that really hadn't entered her mind . . . at least until now.

She fought the need to giggle. Nerves. Had to be nerves. But she felt her labia softening, engorging, knew her clit was beginning to peek out from its little hood of flesh, searching for closer contact with that hot cock. The arms holding her tightened just a bit. One of the hands moved to cover her breast.

Neither one of them spoke. He knew what she looked like. She had no idea who held her. What age he was, what race, what anything.

He saved your life.

There was that. She arched her back, forcing her breast into the huge hand that palmed it. In response, thick fingers compressed the nipple. She bit back a moan. Jared hated it when she made noises during sex.

This isn't Jared, you idiot.

The fingers pinched harder, rolled the turgid flesh between them. *Screw it.* She moaned, at the same time parting her legs just a bit so that she could settle herself on the huge cock that seemed to be growing even larger. Then she tightened her thighs around it, sliding her butt back against his rock-hard belly.

She felt the thick curl of pubic hair tickling her butt, rested against the hard root of his penis where it sprung solidly from his groin and clenched her thighs once again, holding onto him. She felt the air go out of his lungs, then the lightest touch of warm lips against her ear, the soft, exploring tip of his tongue as he circled just the outside, the soft puff of his breath.

Shivers raced along her spine. She wrapped her fingers around his wrists, anchoring herself while at the same time holding both of his hands tightly against her breasts. The hair on his arms was soft, almost silky. She tried to picture her hidden lover, but before an image came to mind, he hmmm'd against her ear, then ran his tongue along the side of her throat.

She felt the sizzle all the way to her pussy, felt his lips exploring her throat, his mobile tongue teasing the wispy little hairs at the back of her neck. His hands massaged her breasts, squeezed her nipples, then rubbed away the pain. His hips pressed against her, forcing his cock to slide very slowly back and forth between her swollen labia.

She moaned again, the sound working its way up and out of her throat before she even recognized it as her own voice. The heat surrounding her intensified. Whoever he was, whoever held her . . . she sighed. He literally radiated fire and warmth and pure carnal lust. One of his big hands slipped down to her belly, cupped her mons and pressed her against him. Still gripping his forearm tightly in her left hand, she felt his finger slide down between her legs.

His fingertip paused at her swollen clit, applying the merest bit of pressure. She held perfectly still, afraid he'd stop if she moved, afraid of her own reaction to this most intimate touch by an absolute stranger. She kept a death grip on the wrist near her breast. The fingers of her right hand dug into the corded tendons on the underside of his forearm, and everything in her cried out to thrust her hips forward, to beg him to stroke her, to bury more than just his finger in the moist heat between her legs.

Instead, as her body trembled with the fierce need to move, she held her hips immobile. After a moment that might have lasted forever, he gently rubbed his fingertip around her clit, dipping inside her wet pussy for some of her moisture, then bringing it back to stroke her once more.

She bit back a scream as his roughened fingertip touched her again, the circular motion so light as to hardly register. Her trembling increased, her desire, her barely controllable need to tilt and force her hips against him, to make him enter her.

She didn't care if he used his cock, his tongue, his finger . . . hell, at this point, he could use his whole fucking hand and it wouldn't be enough. She choked back a whimper as he changed the direction of his massage, moving his fingertip slowly up and down over the small hooded organ. Each stroke took him closer to her pussy. Closer, but not nearly close enough.

Her breath caught in her throat when he dipped inside her, swirled his thick finger around the streaming walls of her pussy, then returned to caress her clit once more. A small part of Xandi's mind reminded her she was being beautifully fucked by a total stranger, that her fingers were clutching thick, muscular arms, that she was clasping her thighs around the biggest cock she'd ever felt in her life—and that they still hadn't exchanged a single word.

It came to her then, in an almost blinding flash of insight, a personal epiphany of pure, carnal need and unmitigated lust, that she'd never, even in her most imaginative fantasy, been this turned on in her entire life. Never felt so tightly linked—mentally, physically, sexually—to anyone. She moaned aloud as his finger once more slipped back between her legs. His thumb stroked her clit now, and that one, thick finger plunged carefully in and out of her weeping flesh.

Suddenly, the hot tip of his tongue traced the whorl of her ear, then dipped inside. Shocked, she thrust her hips forward, forcing his fingers deep. His breath tickled the top of her ear, his tongue swirled the interior, leaving it all hot and damp, filled with lush promise.

She thrust harder against his fingers, still holding one of his hands against her breast, forcing the other deep between her legs. She felt the thick rush of fluid, the hot coil of her climax building, building with each slick thrust of his cock between her thighs, each dip of his fingers, each . . .

Without warning, he rolled her to her stomach, breaking her grip on his forearms as if it were nothing. He grabbed her hips and lifted her. Xandi moaned, spreading her legs wide, welcoming him, begging with her body. Eyes wide open, she saw nothing but darkness, felt no sense of space, lost all concept of time. She quivered, hanging at the precipice of a frightening, endless fall.

His big hands clasped her hips, held her tightly. He massaged her buttocks for a moment with both his thumbs, spreading her cheeks wide. She felt her slick moisture on his fingertip, almost preternaturally aware of each tiny spot on her body where she made contact with his.

She wondered how much he could see, if his night vision were better than hers. It was as dark as the inside of a cave, wherever they were. No matter how hard she tried, she couldn't see the soft bed beneath her, couldn't see her own hands.

Couldn't see his.

Yet the link persisted, the sense of connection, of need, of desire so gut deep it was suddenly part of her existence, of her entire world. A link she knew would be forged forever when he finally entered her, filled her with heat and pulsing need.

He lifted her higher, his hands slipping down to grab her thighs, raising her up so that her knees no longer touched the mattress, so that her weight was on her forearms, her face pressed tightly to the pillow.

She expected his thick cock to fill her pussy. Wanted his cock, now. *Please, now!* Her breath caught in short, wild gasps for air, her legs quivered, and she hung there in his grasp, waiting . . . waiting. Hovering there, held aloft, the cool air drifting across her hot, needy flesh. Waiting for him to fill her.

Instead, she felt him pull away, felt the mattress dip as he shifted his weight . . . felt the fiery wet slide of his tongue between her legs.

"Ahhh . . ." Her cry ended on a whimper. He looped his arms through her thighs and lifted her even higher, his tongue finding entry into her gushing pussy, his lips grabbing at her engorged labia, suckling each fleshy lip into his hot mouth. He nibbled and sucked, spearing her with his tongue, nipping at her with sharp teeth, then laving her with soft, warm strokes. Suddenly his lips encircled her clit, and he suckled, hard, pressing down on the sensitive little organ with his tongue.

The scream exploded out of her. She clamped her legs against the sides of his head, peripherally aware of scratchy whiskers, strong jaw. His tongue lapped and twisted, filling her streaming pussy, as she bucked against him. He was strong, stronger than any man she'd ever known, holding her aloft, eating her out like a hungry beast, his mouth all lips and tongue and hard-edged teeth.

He dragged his tongue across her clit once more, suckled her labia between his lips and brought her to another clenching, screaming climax. Once more, licking her now, long, slow sweeps from clit to anus, each stroke taking her higher, farther. His tongue snaked across her flesh, dipping inside to lap at her moist center, tickling her sensitive clit, ringing the tight sphincter in her ass. Gasping, shivering, her legs trembling, Xandi struggled for breath, reached for yet another climax.

He left her there, once more on the edge. Cool air brushed across her damp flesh, raising goose bumps across her thighs and belly.

He lowered her until her knees once more rested on the bed. She felt his hot thighs pressing against her own, his big hands clasping her hips, the broad, velvety soft tip of his cock resting at the mouth of her vagina.

Slowly, with great care and control, he pushed into her. Damn, he was huge. She shifted her legs, relaxed her spasming muscles as best she could. Still, her flesh stretched, the lubrication from her orgasms easing the way as he slowly, inexorably, seated himself within her.

She felt him press up against the mouth of her womb at the same time his balls nestled against her clit and pubic mound.

He waited a moment, giving her time to adjust to his huge girth and length, then he started to move.

Slowly at first, easing his way in, then out, stretching her, filling her. Xandi fisted the pillow in her hands as she caught his rhythm. In, out, in again, his balls tickling her clit with each careful thrust. She pressed back against him, forcing him deeper, inviting him.

He groaned, then slammed into her harder. She took him, reveled in the power and strength of her mystery lover, felt another climax beginning to build, knew she would not go alone this time.

She reached back between her legs, grasping his lightly furred sac between her fingers just as he thrust hard against her cervix. His strangled cry encouraged her. Grinning, feeling empowered—feminine and so very strong—she squeezed him gently in the palm of her hand, felt his balls contract, tighten, draw up close to his body.

She slipped one finger behind his sac, pressed the sensitive area, then ran her sharp fingernail lightly back to his testicles. He slammed into her, his body rigid with a fierce power. Shouting a warrior's cry of victory, he pounded into her harder, stronger. She kept a tight but careful hold on his balls, until the hot gush of his seed filled her.

Overwhelmed, overstimulated, she screamed and thrust her hips hard against his groin. Her vaginal muscles clamped down, wrapping around his cock, trapping and holding him close. Suddenly, he filled her even more, his cock swelling to fit tightly against the clenching muscles of her pussy, locking his body close against hers.

Linking the two of them together. A binding deeper than the act itself, more powerful than anything she'd ever known.

He slumped across her back, then rolled to his side, taking Xandi with him. She felt the hot burst of his gasping breath, the rhythmic pulsing of his cock, the pounding of her own heart.

Suddenly, inexplicably exhausted, her pussy rippling against the heat of his still amazingly engorged penis, Xandi snuggled close to his rock-hard body and allowed her eyes to drift slowly shut.

Tomorrow. She'd learn who he was tomorrow.

Hot, sexy men come in every shade of fine, and women just have to have them . . . get yours!

GOTTA HAVE IT

by Renée Alexis is available now from Kensington . . .

Marc moved in next to her, lacing his hand up and down the silkiness of her skirt. "Please, Caroline. I really want to be with you now that you're not in my imagination." He slid his hand under her skirt and stroked her smooth upper thighs just above her garter. "You're right here with me, and you smell so damn good." He kissed her earlobe. "Come home with me. I won't force anything on you. We can do whatever you want to do."

The way he was making her feel, she'd have clearly jumped into a pool of stingrays with him. "What . . . what about my ticket?"

He placed the credit card in her hand. "Let's get it changed, and If nothing's available, I'll let you go, or drive you there myself. Please! I want to make love to you so badly that I can taste you. I can still feel your breasts in my hands, your tongue winding around mine. Your flavor is still on my fingers and I'm just shy of sucking them to regain that sensuous aroma."

"Marc . . ." No one alive or dead ever said that to her and in the way he said it. Marc had a way with words and sex, and if his tactics developed the way his body had over the years, she'd never leave Lake Shore Drive. Her life would be spent within his world.

She didn't know if it was her mind playing games with her or if Marc's fingers really found her spot. Without thinking, her hand lowered, landing on top of his and from that point on her hand guided his movements. Her thick moisture saturated both her hand and his as his fingers swirled around her clit, stroking it with smooth, precise caresses. He inched deeper inside filling her. She could hear her own moisture mixing with his movements and the sound alone made her quiver and constrict around him. "Marc, Marc . . . please . . ."

His voice tickled her ears. "Come home with me, Caroline. Take me out of this misery."

The protrusion busting his pants apart beckoned her, and her hand gripped the clothed swollen gland, working it, manipulating it until he could barely stand the pressure. Their mouths met with steam and passion, nibbling on lips separated from each other for way too long. His mouth temporarily broke free from hers, trailing across to her earlobe, then down her neck. His breathy voice pursued. "Let's buy your ticket because that late plane will not be seeing you today."

Without any hesitation, Caroline followed her captor through the bar, leaving a half devoured blue Crush on the table. Hand in hand, they approached the Delta Airlines ticket agent and made the exchange with ease.

With a new departure date the following morning, Caroline happily skipped out of Midway Airport with Marc Brown by her side. They reached his Porsche and she stared in wonder. "You see, this is what money does for you."

"Anytime you want it, it's yours."

She smoothed her hand along the jet-black auto. "No, what I really want is the man driving it. That's all I've ever wanted, Marc."

"Then your life is made because there's no way in fucking

hell you're getting rid of me." He unlocked the door and helped her inside. Her skirt slid up her leg as she entered the vehicle and Marc's tongue practically wagged out of control. *Lord, get me and that girl him fast before I explode!*

the tour along Lake Shore Drive was amazing. She'd seen it many times, but never from Marc's window. It was a beautiful, sunny day, a more perfect day hadn't been created, and what made it absolutely prefect was that she was spending it in Marc's arms. The minute they entered his mansion, she knew she'd wrap herself around him so tightly that they'd make the first human rubberband. She could actually feel Marc sliding that hulking thick meat into her and shattering what was left of her sanity. That was what she needed. No man in her past left an impression upon her the way he did with one evening in a shower. From that point on in her life, wherever she moved to, she made sure the shower was on jam!

Marc took her mind from her bathroom orgasm. "Hey, pretty girl. Whatcha' thinkin' about?"

The side of her dainty little mouth perked up. "I don't think you want to know that."

"Now I really want to know."

Her hand stroked his inner tight. "Well, I was thinking about showers." She faced him bluntly. "And I don't mean rain showers."

"Girl, I like the sound of that. So tell me, what were we doing in the shower?"

"I didn't get into it that deeply, but there's something about showers that turns me out!" Her hand moved from his leg, to his groin, on to his stomach and caressed his chest. He was still so soft, baby flesh, like she remembered from years ago. "You still feel so good."

"I think it's that aftershave I advertise."

"I have seen that commercial. Sexy, sexy as can be."

"So, finish that shower thing you went off on."

"I was just wondering how it would be making love to you in your shower. I'm sure you have many."

"I have four, and I plan to christen you in all of them."

Her hand moved back to his erection, stroking it, making the linen pants material cause friction against it. She loved the way his eyes glowed from her affections; how his muscles tensed, the degree of heat emitting from those pants. Heat wasn't exactly the only thing she wanted from those pants; she wanted fire, steam, white-hot lava and she wanted it dripping slowly and thickly down his shaft. She tugged at his zipper, then eyed him. "May I?"

"God! Yes."

There was no one on the tree-lined street but them and his Porsche, so he pulled to the side of road. "Why wait for the shower when we can get wet right here?"

"Ummm, I like how you talk, Mr. Marc Brown, king of the Sox bullpen."

"I want to be your king, your every-damn-thing, pretty girl!"

With his hand covering hers, they slid his zipper down. Before the zipper was at half-mast, his tight, seething erection was trying to bust apart all that was in its way. To tease Marc into exquisite hardness, her tongue darted at the clothed tip, rubbing wetly against the roughness of the Hanes briefs. Marc was ready to go into spasms just from the friction of underwear and her mouth. The feast d' resistance came when she totally took the covered shaft into her mouth, sucking the damp material, making it cling against his rod.

Watching Caroline dine on him made his breathing quicken, his stomach heaved in and out. Her other hand raised his shirt, stroked soft thick flesh and muscles—taming his breathing. His words worked on her as she worked on him. "Damn, this is so fucking good, Caroline. Don't stop . . . don't stop." He reached down and delivered his shaft from the wet material while reclining the bucket seat.

Exposed to her hungry eyes was a shaft so beautiful and cinnamon brown that she almost came. Her fingers glided up and down the thick, rigid erection as it continued to pulsate. The sight of it took her breath away. It'd been so long since her beloved Marc was in her arms; just knowing she'd never mix with him again, never feel any real love from him. But as she stroked his molten flesh, she knew it was real, Marc was real, and her dreams were about to come true again.

He beckon her. "Take it, darling."

More than just words, it was action. Caroline's mouth started at his tip, feasting on it, tenderizing it before she dove in for the rest. Marc stroked it up and down for her satisfaction, and his, as her mouth sank deeper and deeper in it. His thick veins tickled her inner cheeks and throat and she smiled over the fact that he was still way different from what she remembered in dad's medical book. He was an awakening, then and now.

Marc's hips pumped to her rhythm, forcing the shaft deep within her mouth. She was taking it, taking it all but found her comfort zone at the plump, rounded tip. She sipped him, as though he were a fine wine and watched as he erupted from her hand action. He slumped in the seat, staring at his glorious princess. "You are so incredible, Caroline. How'd you learn to do that?"

"I had a good teacher—you. You made me want to be good at it."

"But we only did it once."

"Good teachers need only teach a lesson once."

He kissed her in a long, sucking motion, getting his fill of her before pulling away. "Sit on me. Let me feel what it's like again to be with you. You were so good."

"I was a virgin."

"That meant you were a natural. Come on, sit on me."